CO-ARA-169

TAKING THE ICE

Lorna Schultz
Nicholson

Cover by
Khaula Mazhar

Scholastic Canada Ltd.
Toronto New York London Auckland Sydney
Mexico City New Delhi Hong Kong Buenos Aires

Scholastic Canada Ltd.
604 King Street West, Toronto, Ontario M5V 1E1, Canada

Scholastic Inc.
557 Broadway, New York, NY 10012, USA

Scholastic Australia Pty Limited
PO Box 579, Gosford, NSW 2250, Australia

Scholastic New Zealand Limited
Private Bag 94407, Botany, Manukau 2163, New Zealand

Scholastic Children's Books
Euston House, 24 Eversholt Street, London NW1 1DB, UK

www.scholastic.ca

Library and Archives Canada Cataloguing in Publication

Title: Taking the ice / Lorna Schultz Nicholson ; cover by Khaula Mazhar.
Names: Schultz Nicholson, Lorna, author.
Identifiers: Canadiana (print) 20210226153 | Canadiana (ebook) 20210226161 |
    ISBN 9781443182393 (softcover) | ISBN 9781443182409 (ebook)
Classification: LCC PS8637.C58 T35 2021 | DDC jC813/.6—dc23

7 6 5 4 3 2 1   Printed in Canada 114   21 22 23 24 25

To kids who deal with anxiety; you're not alone.

CHAPTER ONE

EVERYTHING NEW

Dust covered the photo in Aiden's hands. He wiped the glass with his sleeve, and the dust blew up his nose, making him sneeze. Gross!

"Aiden, your bus is coming down the road," his mom called from the bottom of the stairs. "You better hurry up."

Aiden placed the photo of his father in his Florida Panthers jersey face down on his dresser. Then he went to the bathroom to give his teeth a five-second brush. Outside, the bus honked to tell Aiden he was late. His stomach heaved, and his heart started beating faster.

"Aiden," his mother called again. "Are you okay up there?"

Aiden put down his toothbrush and took the creaky stairs of his grandfather's dusty old house one at time. His feet wouldn't move to "hurry up." At the bottom of the stairs, he picked up his backpack and glanced out the window to see the branches of the bush next door still covered in white. Snow had fallen in September! It was like the weather here went from summer to winter overnight. He shook his head and walked into the kitchen.

"Bus is waiting," said his mother.

"I know," Aiden said quietly.

"Are you okay?" his mom asked. She moved to touch his face.

"Please don't," said Aiden. "I'm fine."

"I had to walk to school," mumbled his grandpa. "Five miles, every day."

As much as Aiden sometimes wanted to tell Grandpa that life wasn't about the olden days anymore, he didn't. It wasn't his grandpa's fault he was old and liked to tell the same stories over and over — or that he was the reason they had to move. Well, one of the reasons. Aiden pushed down the lump in his throat and kissed his grandpa's bristly cheek before walking outside.

The bitter air smacked him in the face. Aiden was sure he would never get used to winter lasting ten times longer than summer. He was still zipping up his too-thin jacket — the one from last year's hockey team in Florida — when he stepped onto the bus and walked past the driver.

"Sorry," said Aiden. He ducked his head.

"You're lucky I knew your dad," said the driver. "Used to watch him play. Man, did he have wheels."

Aiden's throat went dry. His heart accelerated. *Why did everyone always have to mention him?*

All the seats up front were taken, so Aiden kept walking down the aisle, trying to look calm. But his heart was beating out of control, and his stomach churned. *Breathe. Breathe.*

Near the back of the bus, he saw two guys he *sort of* knew: Craig and Jory. Jory gave him a one-finger wave. *Was that an invitation?* They were all in the same sixth-grade class, so he'd met them at school and then again at hockey tryouts, but it's not like they were friends. His stomach did another somersault.

Aiden kept moving his feet, past one row of seats, then another. Kids stared at him. Of all the guys who played hockey at his *new* school, in his *new* minor hockey association, Jory was probably Aiden's favourite. *Would it be okay to sit behind Jory and Craig? Would Craig tell him to get lost, to sit somewhere else?*

Aiden missed his friends in Florida. They knew him, liked him. Aiden had sent them a picture of the snow the night before, and they'd howled, telling him to be Mr. Freeze for Halloween. And then . . . they'd asked about hockey. He'd stickhandled like a dirtbag through his answer in order to avoid the truth.

So far there had been four tryouts, and when it was over, they would make four under-13 teams. The first tryout had been all skating and drills, and the next three tryouts had been scrimmages only. He'd only scored two goals total. Not good. Craig had scored a hat trick in one game. So many kids were trying out, and it was so competitive. Plus, no matter what team he made, Aiden was going to be playing with kids he didn't know. It would be nothing like it was back in Florida.

Aiden inhaled and plopped down behind Jory and Craig. *Hold it in. Act cool. Breathe.*

Jory turned and laughed at him. "Hey, man. Did you just wake up or something?"

Aiden shrugged. "It was warm under the covers."

"You ain't seen nothing yet, wuss," said Craig.

"Last I looked, it's still September," said Aiden. He hoped he sounded tough, that his voice wasn't shaking. Craig O'Brien was a kid Aiden didn't know how to act around.

"Fall, winter — all the same thing here, Mallory," said Jory. "Cold and snowy. Anyway, tomorrow it's October."

"He's from *Flor-i-da* where it never snows." Craig smirked. "This is probably the first snow he's ever even seen." He also talked loudly.

Aiden felt his heart racing. *Was everybody on the bus looking at him?* "I've seen snow," he mumbled. "Just not in September."

"How long you lived here, *Flor-i-dian*? What have you been here, like, two months of your life? Is that your record?" Craig talked even louder now. "You'd think you'd be used to moving by now. My dad said your dad was *always* being traded." His voice carried through the entire bus. Kids turned around. Craig scowled at the ones younger than him, and the not-so-popular kids.

Aiden stared at the floor. He really wanted to tell Craig to *shut up*. If he had the guts to move to another seat, he would have, but instead he mumbled, "We were in Florida for *five* years." Aiden slouched in his seat and stared at the snow that was turning into grey puddles on the filthy bus floor.

Craig stuck his feet up on the back of the seat in front of him. Out of the corner of his eye, Aiden could see the wet snow dripping off Craig's high-top shoes. For sure it would form a puddle on the empty seat. The poor kid who sat there next would end up with a wet butt. None of Aiden's friends in Florida were rude like that.

"I didn't want to get out of bed this morning either, but not because of the snow," said Jory. "I have to present something in class today. I hate talking in front of everyone. I sweat so much my pits get soaked." He flapped his arms up and down.

Aiden managed a laugh. "Oh, *right*. You're up today. I *hate* talking in front of groups too. I get those bad pits."

Why did he say that? Now he was yapping. From one extreme to the next. "Once I tried to dry them under the hand dryer in the restroom before a presentation." *He needed to stop talking.*

Craig shook his head at him. "What a loser thing to do," he said.

Aiden sunk lower in his seat and looked at the dirty bus floor again.

Jory laughed. "I think it's funny. I might try that."

"Not me," said Craig. "I wow the teachers. Just like that." He snapped his fingers.

"Yeah, well, I would rather wow the puck," said Jory. "Last tryout tonight." He shook his head. "I feel like I lost so much with my broken leg last year. That toboggan hill was fun, but not fun enough to miss half a season of hockey. I hope I can make it up tonight."

"I think team phone calls are going out after tonight's tryout, right?" said Aiden.

Craig held up his crossed fingers. "We're like this, me and that puck. I already know I'm making the top team. It'll have the best coach."

Craig was the one guy Aiden's age who might actually make the top U13 team. From what Aiden understood, everyone in the area, even from other towns, tried out for Prairie Field's minor hockey association because it was known for having the most competitive teams.

"Can you believe they let a high-school kid coach one of the teams this year?" Craig continued. "Coach Ira didn't even play juniors. My dad says it's ridiculous. But the guy will probably coach team four, so who cares. What happens on the rec team doesn't affect moi." He raised his eyebrows up and down. "You like my French?"

Aiden had no idea how they picked teams, or who would be on his team or be his coach. All he knew was that players were slotted from best to worst.

"Did you see how I dangled the goalie in our last try-out?" Craig flicked his hair out of his eyes.

"Whatever, O.B." said Jory. He rolled his eyes at Craig.

Suddenly Craig pulled his feet off the seat and sat up straight. "Hey, did you guys hear about what happened at the arena last night?"

"I know U15 tryouts happened. Why, was there a fight?" Jory asked.

"Better. Someone from their tryouts left a bunch of garbage on the floor in the dressing room. Ned lost it big time. I guess he started ranting about RESPECT. Then a few of the parents got revved and there was like an off-ice brawl."

"Punches?" Jory asked.

"Not real punches," said Craig. "My dad said it probably happened because the parents are all so freaked about the arena shutting down part time to cut costs. Our minor hockey organization is brutal right now. The U15 triple A team is a **nightmare**, and without ice time they are soooo going to lose. They better get the upgrades done soon, or my dad says I'm going to a different organization."

Ever since Aiden had moved to Prairie Field in July, he'd heard non-stop about the arena needing new, energy-efficient lights because the old ones cost way too much money to run.

"Can you imagine if parents really were throwing punches?" Jory asked. Then he laughed. "That'd be hilarious. Did they find out who did it?"

"Nope. No one will squeal," said Craig. "I guess there was some 'discussion' after, about Ned, and how he needed to 'relax about the garbage deal.'" Craig rolled his eyes. "It's like cleaning up after everyone isn't his job. Anyway, apparently banana peels are his pet peeve."

For the rest of the bus ride, Aiden didn't say too much. Instead he listened to the chatter and looked out the window at the snow that went on forever. No ocean, no beach, no trees — just kilometres of nothing but white. He thought about Ned, and how his dad always used to visit Ned at the arena when he was in town. Aiden's mom had told him that when Ned was young, he'd had a snowmobile accident that hurt his brain. Physically Ned looked okay, but the accident had changed him. He didn't always react to situations the way other people did. Aiden understood that feeling all too well.

Eventually the bus lurched to a stop in front of the school, and the driver threw the doors open. A cold draft swept down the aisle of the bus. Aiden stood and slung his backpack over his shoulder. *Here goes nothing.*

CHAPTER TWO

THE DEAL

All morning Aiden tried to listen to his teacher, but his mind kept wandering. He tapped his pencil on his desk. Why did they have to move *here*? Once, and only once, he'd asked his mother why Grandpa couldn't move to Florida instead of them moving to Prairie Field, but that went over like a smelly stink bomb. Mom shook her head and said she couldn't fight history and stubbornness, and for the record she wished he would move too, but he wouldn't. Then she'd launched into a long speech about being the only child and only one to take care of him. Aiden's Grandma had passed away years ago, and they'd had his mom when they were super old, like forty. Plus . . . because his mom was Canadian, they couldn't really stay in Florida anymore, not *without Dad*. There were "complications."

"Aiden Mallory, can you please stop tapping your pencil."

Aiden slid down in his seat. Mr. Rowland's comment had made the rest of the class go silent, and Aiden knew they were boring holes in his back. He lowered his head and stared at the top of his desk. His face heated, then scorched. Behind him, the whispers started.

"His dad scored thirty goals one season!"

"Did you hear what actually happened to him though?"

"Yeah. It was all over the news. He blew it big time."

"Leave it alone," said a girl's voice.

"Well, he did go from being a hero to a zero."

"It wasn't true," said the same girl. "What they said on the internet."

"How do you know?"

"I heard there's going to be some tournament named after him." Aiden recognized Craig's voice. "He shouldn't have a tournament. Not after what happened."

"Sure he should. The guy's a legend."

A tournament named after his dad?

Mr. Rowland spoke from the front of the class, jarring Aiden back to reality. "That's enough talking, class. Let's get down to business."

Aiden slouched lower. If he could disappear, he would. Seriously, a tournament named after his father? Where? When? *That would just make everyone talk about his dad that much more.* Aiden hated that they all wanted to know what had happened to him. He didn't want to relive a minute of that nightmare, yet snippets kept coming at him as if they were downloaded into his brain and wouldn't leave.

Finally lunch arrived, and Aiden took out his lunch kit. He found a quiet place to eat by himself so no one would ask him questions — especially about his dad. So often, he just wanted to talk to his dad one more time instead of hearing everyone talk *about* him.

After Aiden finished eating, he went outside. He found another quiet spot and watched the playground action. Mostly seventh graders played at the basketball hoops. The little kids ran around the playground area, which had bars and swings. Kids of all ages kicked soccer balls. But what was completely different at this school was that you could check out plastic hockey sticks and play ball hockey. That would so not happen in Florida. Baseball and basketball were the big sports there. Aiden had been wanting to play ball hockey for weeks but wasn't sure how to get invited. He hung against the wall instead.

The afternoons in class always seemed to go a lot quicker than the mornings. Aiden guessed that was because he had made it through the awkwardness of lunch. English was Aiden's last subject of the day, but with the final tryout looming, he struggled to listen. He clenched his pencil so he wouldn't be tempted to tap it and thought about the new deke he had been practising.

He had to be better in this tryout. He had to score. He focused on his skating, on moving the puck.

But then, suddenly, Mr. Rowland's voice entered his brain cells. "Aiden?"

Aiden looked up.

"Can you repeat what I just said?"

He heard Craig behind him. "Flor-i-dian is busted again."

Aiden's face hit a new shade of red, he was sure, and this time his throat dried up completely, so he just sat there like a stiff. He heard kids around him giggling. Probably laughing at Craig's nickname for him. *When was the bell going to go?*

"I didn't think so," Mr. Rowland said, a little more softly. "Listen up, okay? This is important."

Aiden kept his gaze on Mr. Rowland. He had to.

"For our first English assignment of the year," Mr. Rowland said, "you will be writing a personal essay. It will have to be in essay style, which is what we have been going over for the past few weeks."

Many kids in the class groaned. Aiden didn't join in, although he would have loved to. Personal? He didn't want to write anything personal. *His essay would suck.*

Mr. Rowland continued talking. "There are going to be steps to this writing assignment, and each will have to be handed in."

He wrote the word *outline* on the board. "First is the outline. And it will be worth twenty percent. I want to see a description of your topic and a list of the three points you will be writing about in this essay."

Then Mr. Rowland started droning on about picking something with significance to write about. It could be serious or funny. Aiden's life had nothing in it that was funny right now. He jiggled his leg. He guessed he could write about playing hockey in Florida versus playing hockey in Prairie Field, and the pros and cons of each.

"And, hockey boys — and girl." Mr. Rowland smiled at a girl named Susie. "Let's try to think of something besides hockey, unless it has significant personal meaning. I don't just want a story about why you want a certain team to win the Stanley Cup. Or how your favourite player scored the most goals. Or how *you* scored a gazillion goals last season. It needs something personal to go along with it."

Aiden heard the snickers behind him. Then he heard Jory say, "If only I could score a gazillion goals."

Aiden figured he could also write about how it sucked to move. That had *significance.* Maybe he would just write about how bad his life was and see what Mr. Rowland thought about that. Either way, he knew the one thing he *wouldn't* write about.

When the school bell rang, Aiden was so relieved. Over, for one more day. On the bus ride home he nabbed a front seat and sat by himself. Jory and Craig were at the back of the bus with their hockey friends. The bus buzzed with talk about the final tryout. Who would make what team. Coaches. Tournaments. Everything. All day at school Aiden had wanted to ask someone about the tournament that was supposedly going to be named after his father. *Did his mother know? Did she just not tell him?*

Aiden's stomach did its pre-tryout flip-flops. Hockey. Hockey. Hockey. That's all the kids talked about. The bus dropped Aiden off in front of his house, and he hurried to get inside.

"Hey, Mom!" he yelled from the mud room.

There was no answer. He called again. Still no answer. He headed into the kitchen to get some food and then he saw the note.

Hi Aiden,
I had to take Grandpa to a doctor's appointment. We'll be home around four thirty. We need to leave by six for your tryout. We're having spaghetti tonight to give you energy. Be ready to eat at five thirty.
Love, Mom

Since his mom wasn't home, he didn't have to do his homework right this minute. That was also something new: his mother leaving him alone for an hour.

She said she felt safer in Prairie Field, but Aiden didn't. He didn't want to be in this creepy old house by himself. He put his coat back on and got his street-hockey stick and a bucket of pucks from the shed, then he ran all the way to the arena. Today it had been closed in the morning but was opened at noon, and he wanted to practise shooting before the tryout tonight.

When he arrived, the lobby was spotted with parents and figure skaters. He headed straight to the practice-shooting area, hoping no one else had the same idea as him. Aiden breathed a sigh of relief when he saw the area was empty. He dumped his pucks onto the concrete, lined them up, and started taking wrist shots to warm up. He was on his second round when he heard a voice behind him.

"Whaaatcha doing?"

Aiden immediately turned to see Ned grinning at him. Aiden didn't know how old Ned was but thought his wrinkled face looked like an old baseball glove that was comfortable and well worn, especially when he smiled. Like the older people in Florida, he looked like he had a tan summer and winter. Ned was wearing the same green-and-black lumber jacket he'd worn every day since the hockey season had started, along with his Florida Panthers ball cap. Aiden's dad had signed the hat and given it to Ned on one of his visits. A lot of kids laughed at Ned because he fixated on things like keeping the arena clean and wore the same hat and jacket every day.

"Hi, Ned," said Aiden.

"Your daddy used to come in here and . . . practise too." Ned sometimes talked slowly, and it could take him a second to find a word, almost as if his brain had to think about it first.

"My dad?"

"Yup, your daddy."

Ned walked toward Aiden, pretending to stickhandle. When he was close, he wound up, swinging his arm back as if he was taking a shot. Then he did a fake shot and yelled, "He scores!"

"Top corner," said Aiden.

"Your daddy gave me his first NHL hat trick puck."

"He did?"

"Oh yeah. I have it on a . . . shelf. Your daddy scored a lot of goals when he played for Prairie Field. So many goals. Could he ever pop that puck in the net. Holy Hannah!"

"So I've been told." Aiden stickhandled with the puck. "My grandpa tells me every day." He lowered his head. "And so does everyone else around here." Aiden paused for a second. Then he asked, "Hey, do you know anything about some tournament named after him?"

Ned avoided eye contact with Aiden. "I know nothing about that," he said.

Aiden could tell by the sheepish look on Ned's face that he definitely knew something.

Ned patted his chest. "If it's true — which I don't know anything about — your daddy deserves it."

So it *was* true.

Ned wound up for another fake shot on net. "Sometimes I'd let him go on the ice if no one was here. He'd come early in the morning when it was still dark outside."

Ned looked around as if he didn't want anyone to hear what he was going to say next. Then he turned back to Aiden. "I could sneak him on. I got . . . keys. I would put on goalie pads and stop his shots." He grinned and wound up again. "He blasted them through the air, but I stopped them. Well, maybe not all of them." He laughed. "He always said I . . . helped him."

Aiden stared at Ned. "*You* put on goalie pads and stopped *my dad's* shots?"

"You betcha."

"That's so cool," said Aiden.

"He had such a quick . . . release," said Ned. Once again, he got in position and mimicked shooting the puck. "When it landed on his stick, he just snapped it. I would feed him the puck and he would snap away." Ned laughed again. "We always said he was like a camera. Snap, snap."

Aiden knew that about his father. The sports reporters always talked about it. His dad was the star here in Prairie Field, but in the NHL he had been a third-line specialist because of his snap shot from the slot.

Ned stood up tall. "He would get put on the power play because he had that shot."

"That's true," said Aiden. "Wish I had a shot like that," he mumbled. "Might help me make a good team."

"It's all about practising," said Ned.

"That's for sure," said Aiden. He wished he could get that kind of extra practice his dad had. Learn a specialty that made him good. Make people talk about *his* hockey skills.

Have a tournament named after him.

Ned glanced around, then he turned to Aiden. "Probably best if you don't say nothing about him and me going on the ice. It was a long time ago, but still."

"I won't," said Aiden. Who would he tell, anyway? The wall? It's not like he had a lot of friends here. And his friends in Florida wouldn't care. They didn't even know Ned. Then Aiden had an idea. What if he—

"I gotta go," Ned said, interrupting Aiden's thought.

Ned pointed to a young girl pulling a bag behind her. "Figure skaters today. They need the ice in tip-top shape, no . . . ruts or else they fall. And I don't want no falling. But you can stay here and practise."

Aiden stopped moving and looked right at Ned. "Maybe we could go on the ice too? Like you did with my dad."

Ned's eyes widened and he whispered. "Me and you?"

"Yeah," said Aiden quietly.

"I don't know about that," said Ned. He shook his head. "It's so busy when the arena is open, and I got to keep . . . buzzing around like a bee. All the extra shutdowns make it hard because the ice is . . . booked right up."

Aiden shrugged. "I just thought it might help me be better," he said. "Like it did with my dad. I need the extra practice too."

"Well, maybe it would be all right."

"Maybe we could go early in the morning? I'd be up for that. That way we won't interrupt anything else going on."

"They got light problems in this here arena," said Ned. "When the rink is closed, it's . . . supposed to be *closed*. No games, no practices, no . . . nothing."

"Yeah, I know that," said Aiden. "But thirty minutes can't hurt. Right?"

Ned frowned as if he was thinking. Then he nodded and said, "I guess you're right. Can't hurt. And I still got my goalie pads."

"Do we have a deal?" Aiden stuck out his hand, and Ned shook it.

"It's a deal," said Ned.

CHAPTER THREE

FINAL TRYOUT

"You didn't eat much," said Aiden's mom. She pointed to the spaghetti still left on his plate.

"I can't," said Aiden.

"Try to eat a little more."

Aiden shook his head. "I'll puke." He pushed his plate away, then looked at his mom. "Do you know about some tournament named after Dad?"

Her face went all serious. "Where did you hear about that?" she asked.

So it was true. "At school," he said.

She shook her head and sighed. "Nothing stays secret in this town. I remember that from when I was growing up — everyone knows everything about everybody. Yes, there's going to be a tournament. I was planning to tell you after tryouts were over."

"What teams are involved?"

"All the U13 from Prairie Field and the surrounding communities, except for the rec teams. If it goes well, next year they will expand it to the U15 as well. They want to make it a weekend event, to raise some money for the lights."

"So, I'd have to play in it?" Aiden spun his fork around.

"Yes, that was the plan. They wanted my permission to use Dad's name. I'm also going to be on the fundraising committee for it. But it hasn't been officially announced yet, so please don't say anything to anyone."

Aiden sucked in a deep breath. "What if I make the rec team, Mom?" He got up from the table. "That will be so embarrassing. My dad has a tournament named after him, and I'm so lousy I don't get to play in it."

"Aiden, don't think that way," said his mother. "You've been doing fine out there." She tried to hug him.

He moved away from her. He needed to stay un-emotional, not think about his dad, not think about the tournament.

One more tryout. *One more.* He had to make the one or two team. *He had to.* He couldn't make the recreational team. *What would his Florida friends think? What would Grandpa think? And the kids at school?* The only person who would say it was okay was his mother.

"Can you save my dinner? I'll eat after."

Aiden's mother nodded. His grandfather slurped a strand of spaghetti, and sauce flew everywhere, creating a tomato shower. *Ewwww.* Aiden backed away from the table.

"Can we leave in ten, Mom? I'd like to be there early."

"It's good to get to the arena early," said Grandpa. He looked up at Aiden and wiped his mouth. "When I was a coach, that was important. Show up early and ready to play. Luke did that."

Aiden stiffened at the mention of his dad's name. "Yeah, so I've been told," he said.

Aiden had also been told his father had always made the top team, been the fastest skater, the highest scorer, the captain . . . the list went on and on. And now there was going to be a tournament. *What if he messed up and couldn't play in it? Or what if he played in it and sucked?*

"He was always at the rink before I even got there," said Grandpa. "He always practised, took shot after shot against the wall. Best player I ever coached."

Aiden's mother looked at Aiden and gestured to the stairs. Aiden left the room to get ready. Five minutes later, he had his hockey bag packed and was waiting in the car. His leg jiggled up and down and he couldn't stop it. The snow had almost disappeared, so at least he wasn't shaking from freezing — no, just nerves.

When his mom got in the car, he said, "Is Grandpa going to be okay alone?"

"I talked to the neighbours, and they'll check on him."

"I guess that's one good thing about living in a

small town," said Aiden. He played with the ties on his hoodie.

"I know this adjustment has been hard on you." His mother backed out of the driveway and onto the road.

"I don't want to talk about it," said Aiden. "I just want to focus on this last tryout. So much is going on, and I can't make that rec team, Mom. I just can't. How embarrassing would it be if I didn't play in my *dad's* tournament."

"Just do your best and you'll be fine."

"I don't even know what my best is anymore." Aiden stared out the window.

It took all of three minutes to get to the arena, and Aiden's mother dropped him off at the front doors. The arena was like an old barn and not modern at all. It was no surprise it needed new lights. Aiden didn't talk to anyone as he made his way to the bulletin board where the dressing-room assignments were posted. As he was looking for his name, he felt a jolt to his back.

"Hey, Little Mallory, you ready for tonight?"

Aiden turned. One of the older players was also looking at the board. He was almost a head taller than Aiden and was standing with a kid who was Aiden's age but went to a different school.

"Hope so," Aiden said.

"Too bad you're not as good as your dad. We'd kill

everyone, like they used to when he played here. Maybe we'd even win provincials."

Red crept from Aiden's neck to the tips of his ears, and heat blasted through his pores. He ducked his head into his coat collar and made his way down the hall to dressing room two. He didn't dare look up because he knew the walls were plastered with photos of his dad. When Aiden got to the right door, he pushed it open and walked into the sparsely occupied room. Good thing — he could get a seat. Last week the room had been so packed he'd had to squeeze onto the edge of a bench.

He started to dress, putting on his equipment piece by piece. His stomach still hadn't settled, and now he was starting to sweat in all the wrong places. *Hold it together.* As he dressed, guys entered the room. No one said anything to Aiden. When he was in his full gear, he leaned back against the wall and jiggled his leg. Up and down. Up and down.

Finally, one of the coaches came in and said, "Listen up!"

Aiden sat up straight and sucked in a deep breath. He could do this. His body wouldn't stop shaking. He would get out there and score and make plays and skate as hard as he could and show them all he deserved to be on one of the top teams.

"It's only scrimmage tonight," said the coach. "I'm

going to read off the list and what bench you're on and what colour pinny you're wearing. Pick it up on the way out. Some of you may not see a lot of ice, so make it count when you do."

After he had read the lists, the coach left the room. The chatter started, and Aiden heard a few guys talking beside him.

"They've slotted guys already. Some aren't even dressing because they've made it."

"I heard ten."

"That means less players, more ice time."

Aiden saw Jory across the room, but they didn't even exchange hellos. Aiden picked up his stick and filed out of the dressing room.

When he hit the ice, he skated the first corner with his stick across his back to stretch out a little bit. He knew there wasn't a lot of time before the whistle went, so he picked up the pace on his second lap, using his edges to do crossovers as he went around the corners. He loved the sound of blades crunching through the ice and pucks smacking against the boards. Everything felt so familiar.

He snuck in two more laps before he heard the whistle. Immediately, Aiden skated toward his assigned bench. When he sat down, he noticed Susie from his class sitting to his right. There were five girls trying out, and one of the seventh graders was so good she was going to make the top team for sure. On Aiden's other side was a kid named J.J., who he also recognized from school.

"Good luck today," said Susie.

Her voice. Aiden glanced at Susie, and it hit him that she was the one who had stuck up for him when everyone was talking about his dad in class. But Aiden didn't want to think about him. Not now.

Go away, Dad.

"Um, you too," said Aiden, his voice cracking.

"At this point I don't care what team I make," she said. "I just want to get the season started. Once you're on a team, you're on a team and then it's all fun."

That wasn't how Aiden felt. Before today's news of the tournament, he had wanted to make one of the top two teams to save face with his old friends. But now he *had* to make a non-rec team so he could at least play in the tournament. The one team was a stretch, but the two team was doable. Could he do it? Prove he could maybe be like his dad one day? Stop the comparisons about how he wasn't?

The first lines hit the ice, and Aiden watched the play from the bench. When he heard his line called, he got ready to hop over the boards for his shift.

"Next line out," said the coach.

Aiden took the ice and skated toward the faceoff zone in his team's end. He was playing centre, so he knew he had to win this faceoff. When he lined up, however, he saw who he was against: the guy who had poked him in the lobby.

Aiden crouched over and placed one hand on the bottom of his stick, staring at the puck in the referee's hand. He waited, watching. His dad had taught him this. The puck dropped while Aiden was thinking of his dad. Aiden batted at it, but the big player shoved him. Aiden tried to hold his ground and hoped one of his wingers would come and snatch the puck. But it got loose and headed toward the boards. Aiden spun around just as the opposing team's defence blasted the puck toward the net. The shot was hard and low. Aiden's goalie didn't have a chance.

Aiden closed his eyes for a moment and exhaled. *That was not good.* They had scored a goal just seconds after the puck had dropped. *He had to be better.* All the coaches would be putting a tick by his name, and it wouldn't be a good one. *He was a minus one already.* Aiden's shoulders slumped as he skated to centre ice.

At the next faceoff, he managed to get a piece of the puck. This time Susie was playing right wing and moved in to pick it up. Aiden took off down the ice, pushing his legs, looking for a pass. When the puck came his way, he scooped it up and, seeing his left-winger open, rifled off a saucer pass. The puck landed in front of J.J., who reached for it but then caught an edge and fell.

A player from the other team nabbed the puck. Aiden stopped and turned, giving chase. He closed the gap, but the player took a weak shot on net. Fortunately, this time the goalie for Aiden's team made the save.

Aiden skated to the bench with Susie. "I wasn't very good," he said to her.

"No big deal," she said.

"I think it is," muttered Aiden.

The next time his name was called, he stepped on the ice determined to play better. He was lined up against the same guy.

"Hey, *Little Mallory*," the player hissed at Aiden. Then he patted his winger on the shoulder. "I'll pop it over to you, 'cause *Little Mallory* won't have a chance."

"Too bad he's not as good as his daddy was," the winger said.

Aiden blew out nervous air. *He had to focus.* But he saw his dad's face in his mind just as the puck dropped. *Go away, Dad.* Aiden tried to get the puck, but he got elbowed in the jaw instead. Aiden glanced at the ref, wondering if he'd call the elbow, but no. Just like they'd planned, the winger from the other team picked up the puck and skated down the ice. Aiden chased him, skating hard, but the winger made a great pass and there was a hard shot on net. The goalie made the save, the whistle blew, and Aiden's line was called off.

For the rest of the scrimmage, Aiden played hard, but he knew he didn't flash and dash enough. He was pushed off the puck more than a few times. And he didn't score — or even get an assist. Something felt off, he kept seeing his dad's face, and he knew he hadn't played his best. Not even close. When the buzzer sounded to end the ice session, he knew there was no chance he was getting a spot on the top team.

As Aiden left the ice, he saw Mr. O'Brien, Craig's dad, up against the glass, scowling. Aiden had noticed that Craig wasn't put on the top lines today, not once.

Aiden headed to the dressing room, where he quietly undressed before going out to the lobby. He saw Jory and wanted to talk to him but . . . *should he?* Jory must have seen him staring because he looked at Aiden and waved. Then he walked over.

"So," said Jory, "guess we find out tonight."

"Yeah," said Aiden.

Jory leaned his cheek against his stick. "Some of the guys in grade seven are huge. I didn't score tonight. I didn't play very well. I missed so much last year that I'm still trying to find the click."

"I'm with ya," said Aiden. "I couldn't do anything out there either."

"O.B. should make the two team for sure," said Jory. "And he might squeak onto the one team, although I think only one of us eleven-year-olds will make that team. For his sake I hope he does though. His father will freak if he doesn't."

"Yeah, he seems pretty intense," said Aiden.

Jory opened his eyes wide. "Pretty intense?! One year he got in a fight in the stands."

"Seriously?" Aiden asked.

"No lie. Someone said something, and he went ballistic. Plus he's been kicked out a few times by the refs."

Aiden saw his mother waving to him. She was standing with Ned, who gave Aiden a thumbs-up.

"I gotta go," Aiden said. "I'll see you tomorrow. Good luck."

"Yeah, you too," said Jory. "Give me your number. I'll text you when I find out. Maybe we'll be together on the two team. My parents aren't real hockey parents, and they always say it's better to be on a team with friends. But . . . that said, I still want to make at least team two."

"I agree," said Aiden. *Did Jory really think of him as a friend?*

After they had plugged each other's number into their phones, Jory tilted his head and looked at Aiden. "I thought you'd be more like O'Brien because your dad was in the NHL."

"Nah," said Aiden. The lump formed in his throat, and he looked away. "Uh, I better go."

"Later," said Jory.

Aiden walked over to his mother. Ned was gone, which was too bad. Aiden had wanted to talk to him about going on the ice. He desperately needed extra practice.

"How do you think you did?" his mother asked.

"Awful," said Aiden. "I don't want to talk about it."

They headed outside. When they were close to the car, his mother said, "No matter what, once you get on a team, you'll have a good year."

No matter what? What was *that* supposed to mean? *Did she know something he didn't?*

CHAPTER FOUR

PHONE CALL

Aiden was pretending to eat his leftover spaghetti, twirling it around his fork, when the call came on the landline — the one his grandpa insisted on keeping like they were from the dinosaur era. Aiden ran to it and picked up after the third ring.

"Hello?" he said.

"Aiden? This is Coach Ira!"

Coach Ira? That was the high schooler! *Oh no. He had made the recreational team.* Any spaghetti Aiden had managed to eat was starting to come back up his throat.

"Um, hi," said Aiden.

"I'm thrilled you're on my team. I know you are going to be a huge asset."

Coach Ira sounded like he was reading right from a coaching manual.

"Um," Aiden mumbled. "So I'm on the rec team?"

"Oh, sorry, no," said Coach Ira. "You're on team three."

Aiden breathed a sigh of relief. He wasn't on the

recreational team. But then it hit him: he wasn't on team one or two either.

"I'm super excited to get started, so we have ice time tomorrow," said Coach Ira. "I've also got our name in for early ice time on Thursday. They are doing morning slots on a lottery system because of the cutbacks."

"Okay," said Aiden.

Coach Ira went on about the team and practices, and Aiden tried to listen, but it was hard. Something inside him deflated like a balloon losing air. He had known he wasn't going to make team one, and he was relieved that he wasn't on the rec team, but . . . he had made the *three team*? His eyes got scratchy and he could feel tears welling up. He turned his body toward the wall and swiped at them.

Coach Ira said, "I'm looking forward to practice tomorrow."

"What time?" Aiden managed to squeak out his words.

"Five p.m. I'll have a schedule of all our ice times on the team website. We have a game coming up in two weeks, and I'm trying to get ice in some out-of-town arenas because our home ice is so scarce. Parents might have to pay extra though."

"I'm sure it will be okay with my mom," Aiden said.

"I've also been in meetings for a super-cool, and

unbelievably exciting, tournament that Prairie Field is going to host," said Coach Ira. "Might even become an annual. Right now it's only for the U13s. And you especially will be beyond pumped when it gets announced."

"Okay." Aiden didn't say anything else, even though he knew what Coach Ira was talking about. At least he would get to play in it. *But what if he was lousy in the tournament, just like he was in tryouts?*

Coach Ira talked for a few more minutes. After Aiden hung up, he didn't want to talk to anyone else, but his mother was leaning against the kitchen counter, facing him. Fortunately, Grandpa was in the living room watching television with the volume blasting.

"So . . ." said his mom.

"Um, team three," said Aiden.

"That's great, Aiden," said his mother. She smiled at him.

"No. It's. Not." Aiden shook his head. "I hate it here. I don't want to be on a team with no friends. Or play in a tournament named after Dad. Everyone is going to say how lousy I am. Everyone will compare me to him. Everything in this stupid town is all about Dad!"

Aiden's mother walked over and put her arm around him. "I know how hard it is to be here." She stroked his hair. "We're reminded of him all the time. But you are your own person, Aiden. Your path will be different, and that's okay. This is your first year here. They've never seen you play, or know your work ethic, and that makes it so much harder to make one of the top teams. Give it time. You've been through a lot, and you don't need to be so hard on yourself. This is only one year, and you'll make new friends — no matter what team you're on."

His mom hugged him, and he let her. After a couple of seconds, she said, "Your dad would be proud of you. You know that, right?"

Aiden laid his head against her shoulder, and she felt comfortable and soft, like his Florida Panthers blanket. The thought of that blanket made his emotions kick into high gear. How many times had his mom hugged him just like this since last April? Patted his back. Told him everything would be okay even when she was crying too. Aiden's tears started. *Stupid tears.* He hated them, but ever since his dad's death, he didn't know how to stop them. They rolled down his cheeks and splashed against his mother's sweatshirt.

"I want to talk to Dad." He couldn't hold it in any longer. The faucet had been turned on. His shoulders started to shake. "I wish he was here."

His mother hugged him tighter. "Me too," she

whispered. She kissed the top of Aiden's head. "Me too. Every minute of every day."

Aiden inhaled to catch his breath and stop the sobs. He didn't want to start hyperventilating. Been there, done that. And more, including the freaky panic attacks. *The meltdowns.* Aiden's mom wiped his cheeks with her fingers, then pulled Aiden back into her embrace.

"We'll be okay," she said, as Aiden rested his cheek against her again. "We have each other."

As they were hugging, Grandpa belched from the living room. Then he farted, and it sounded like a loud horn.

Suddenly, Aiden went from crying to laughing. "And we have Grandpa," he said.

His mother laughed along with him. "We sure do."

* * *

When Aiden got on the bus the next morning, he saw Jory and Craig, but they didn't wave to him. Jory hadn't texted him the night before either. *So much for being friends.* There were no seats at the front of the bus, so he had no choice but to walk by them.

"Hey," said Jory, as Aiden got close. "Grab a seat."

Aiden slid into the empty seat across from Jory and Craig. Craig sat by the window, sunk down in his seat with his chin hitting his chest. His baseball hat was lowered over his eyes, so Aiden couldn't see his face.

Obviously, he hadn't made team one. Aiden thought he might as well get his own news out in the open.

"I made team three," he said, as quickly as he could.

"Me too," said Jory. "I'm choked. I was hoping for at least two. I didn't text you because I was so rattled with the call."

Craig didn't say anything and instead looked out the window, pulling the brim of his cap even lower. Jory looked over at Aiden and discreetly pointed to Craig, then held up three fingers. Aiden stared at him wide-eyed. Craig had made team three too? That was unbelievable. Aiden thought he should have been on at least team two for sure.

For the rest of the bus ride, Aiden and Jory spoke a bit about who else might be on their team, but Aiden didn't know many of the names. Some were from the other schools in the area.

Craig didn't say one word until the bus was finally at school. Then he stood up and said, "My dad's gonna fight to get me off your team. It's such a joke."

Neither Jory nor Aiden replied as they all headed off the bus. Craig kept his head down as he walked to class. Aiden and Jory followed a few paces behind.

"I think he's on team three *because* of his dad," whispered Jory.

Aiden just nodded. According to Aiden's mother, his

own dad's father had been like Mr. O'Brien, maybe even worse. Aiden's dad had moved away from his parents when he was young and lived with his uncle in Prairie Field so he could play hockey without his dad yelling at him from the stands and hitting him if he didn't score. Aiden couldn't imagine his dad *ever* hitting him.

"Our coach is new and still in high school," Jory continued, talking quietly. "And I think no one else wanted O.B.'s dad, so they just put him on three because Coach Ira has no idea what he's like." Jory shook his head. "*And* maybe that's even why this Ira guy is coaching team three. Craig's way too good for the rec team, and some high-school guy is not going to be ready to coach the one or two teams."

"Disaster," said Aiden. "Craig should be slotted where he deserves to be."

"Could be a long year," said Jory. "I sure hope I'm wrong and he gets moved up soon. It's going to be nasty if he doesn't."

Aiden didn't reply. Right now, everything seemed nasty.

* * *

During science class, Aiden got paired with Susie to do an experiment.

"What team did you get put on?" she asked. Everyone had been talking — on the playground, in the halls, on the bus and *everywhere* — about who had made what team. Some kids were happy, some were sad and some, like Craig, were furious.

"Three," said Aiden.

"Me too!" She held up her hand for a high-five, and because of her enthusiasm, Aiden had to slap it. Then she laughed and did a dance move that involved swirling her arms around and around. Her long dark braid swung back and forth like a windshield wiper. "I didn't make team four," she sang to her movements.

Aiden burst out laughing despite himself. "I guess I'm glad the teams are finally picked," he said. "I hate try-outs."

"Me too! I get so flippin' nervous. Like, I almost get hives."

"How can you *almost* get hives? You either get them or you don't."

"I get itchy. And I have to scratch like a dog with fleas."

"I guess we have practice at five tonight," said Aiden. Enough of the hive talk. He'd seen his mother's red splotches after his dad had died. "Um, it will be good to get on the ice and just do drills."

"For sure, and I think our coach will be fun," said Susie. "He's young and keen and totally hip. At least that's what my uncle said. Yup, he used the word 'hip.' He said it was good I got someone fresh. I told him I wasn't being coached by a piece of meat." She snorted. "Get it?"

"Yeah, I get it." Aiden smiled. For some reason, Susie's happiness and positive energy about the situation lightened Aiden's mood. They finished their experiment and wrote up the lab notes together.

"Job done," said Susie, as the recess bell clanged. "And just in time. I'm starving. Recess is the best part of the day — well, except lunch."

Like a whirling blur, she was gone, running out the door. Aiden slammed his books shut and shoved them under his desk, then went to get his coat. He didn't move as quickly as Susie. Recess was not his favourite time.

He walked slowly to the back doors. Once he was outside, Aiden shoved his hands in his pockets, trying to look cool. *Where was Jory?* When Aiden saw him hanging out with Craig and a few of the guys who had made higher teams, he decided not to go over. They were probably talking about how Craig got ripped off.

As Aiden was standing around feeling like a loner, two other kids from his class, J.J. and Manny, came up to him.

"Hey, I think we might all be on the same hockey team," said Manny. His name was Emmanuel, but kids called him Manny. Aiden had also heard them call him other names, like Pudgster and Doughboy.

"I'm on team three. What about you guys?" Aiden asked.

"Three," said J.J. Out of his equipment, he was skinny and his jet-black hair was tied up in a sky-blue patka. "I'm so pumped."

"I thought for sure I was making the rec team," said Manny. "But this year I kinda wanted to be on a higher team and play more." Manny's curly blond hair sprung all over the place as he talked.

"We have our first practice tonight," said J.J.

"Yeah," said Aiden. "Did Coach Ira talk to you about early morning practices? I think he's trying to get one."

"Killer," said Manny. "I hate getting up early. I might skip those ones."

"Manny, you can't just skip," said J.J. He playfully slapped him on the shoulder.

"Yeah, probably not a cool thing to do," said Aiden. He couldn't believe someone was already talking about not going to practice. In Florida parents drove hours to take kids to practice and no one ever missed. Ice time was scarcer than here, and coaches nabbed it whenever they could, no matter how far the drive. Plus, parents paid big time.

"My mom said I can if I want to," said Manny.

"You made the *three team*," J.J. said, as if this was the

most amazing thing in the world. "You have to make every practice."

Aiden didn't say much more as J.J. and Manny kept arguing about being committed. Fortunately, the bell rang, and all they walked in together.

When Aiden was hanging up his coat, Jory came over to him. "I saw you talking to J.J. and Manny," he said.

Aiden shrugged. "They did most of the talking. Looks like we're on the same team as them."

"I've never been on a team with either of them before — they've always played rec hockey. O'Brien's so mad he's with them. What a disaster." Jory pretended to smack his head against the lockers.

"Anyone can get better, and sometimes kids like Manny grow to be six-foot-four," Aiden said.

"Yeah. Maybe. Let's hope so for his sake."

"Maybe Craig will get moved up," Aiden said. "Let's hope for that first."

"Yeah, well, we'll see. Attitude counts for something, and right now he's got a baaaaad one. Like, the worst. I can hardly stand talking to him. Blah, blah, blah, blah, blah."

Someone behind Aiden coughed. He turned to see Mr. Rowland standing at the classroom door. "Um, boys?" the teacher said. "Were you thinking of coming to class?"

As Aiden and Jory walked by him to get into the classroom, he added, "Leave the hockey talk in the hallway, okay, boys? Otherwise it's going to be a long year."

The way things were going, Aiden thought it was going to be a long year no matter what.

CHAPTER FIVE

FIRST PRACTICE

That evening Aiden arrived at the arena early for practice and went straight to his team's assigned dressing room. Coach Ira was standing outside the door, holding a clipboard and pen. He wore a track suit that said *Prairie Field High Cougars* and high-top running shoes with untied laces. Earbuds hung around his neck. Aiden had always liked his own brown hair cut short, but Ira had black shoulder-length hair that flipped around his face. Aiden had never had a young coach before, much less one who looked like he belonged in a boy band.

"Aiden!" Coach Ira said. "Congrats on making team three. Glad to see you're early. I like that enthusiasm." His voice sounded like soda bubbles popping, and his eyes were shining like they were doing happy dances. He held up his hand for a high-five.

"Um, thanks," said Aiden. He high-fived Coach Ira back, which was so weird. On his old teams those were saved for goals on the ice.

Aiden was the first person in the dressing room, so he took a plastic ball from his bag and started shooting it against the wall. He got to fifty shots before he heard the door open.

The boy who came in was almost a head taller than Aiden and lugged a massive bag, so he was obviously a goalie. Aiden recognized him as one of the seventh graders he had seen playing basketball at school. A second-year player made the three team? He took his jacket off and hung it up. Muscles, real muscles, showed through his T-shirt.

"Hey," said Aiden, putting his ball back in his bag.

"Hey," said the boy. "Name's Mike, a.k.a. Tree."

"Tree?"

"Yeah. I grew in like grade five. Name stuck." He sat down on the bench. "I'm okay with it. Could be worse."

Aiden stepped forward and stuck out his hand. "I'm Aiden." His nickname in Florida had been Malley, but Aiden didn't want anyone to know him by his last name. Not here.

They shook hands, and Mike/Tree said, "Yeah, I know your name. Everyone does. Um, sorry about your dad."

So much for being anonymous.

"Thanks." Aiden sat down by his bag and tried to look busy pulling out his shoulder pads. No one ever just said anything like that to him about his dad. Usually when dads came up around Aiden, people stopped talking and looked totally uncomfortable. Even adults. In a way, he liked how Tree had acknowledged his dad.

"You go to Prairie Field School, right?" Aiden asked.

"Yeah. I'm probably gonna be the oldest kid on this team. I have a January birthday and I'm in grade seven. But I didn't start playing until I was ten." He shrugged, looking totally okay with the situation. "I'm happy I'm not on team four because that's for players who just want to have fun. I say good for them, but it's just not me. Not anymore. I hope this team is committed, and that everyone cares. Look out next year."

"I hope everyone cares too," said Aiden. He looked at Tree. "Let's make that happen."

"You're on." Tree gave Aiden a thumbs-up.

Soon enough the room filled up. J.J. and Manny bopped in, both pumped. J.J. started getting dressed right away, but Manny sat there talking away to J.J. as he wrapped his stick randomly, the tape going everywhere.

Three kids that Aiden didn't recognize entered the room next. They were chatting comfortably with each other, so Aiden figured they were all from the same school, maybe one outside of Prairie Field, or maybe a private or religious school. He listened to them talking and heard that one of their names — or maybe it was a nickname — was Deke.

A small kid who was in Aiden's class walked in alone.

Aiden thought he would look like a little kid next to Tree. Like Manny, he was a playground target, but Aiden couldn't remember his name. He closed his eyes and tried to hear Mr. Rowland's voice talking to the boy in class, but what came to Aiden was not Mr. Rowland. It was the kids on the playground calling him Baby Bilal. Aiden watched as Bilal squeezed himself into a spot on the bench.

Within a few minutes three more kids had walked in together. Aiden wondered if there were any girls besides Susie on the team. Of course, they would be dressing in a different room, so he'd have to wait to find out. When Aiden saw Jory enter, he moved over so Jory could sit beside him if he wanted.

"Have you seen O.B. yet?" Jory asked, as soon as he plunked himself down.

Aiden shook his head. "Not yet."

Jory glanced around the room, then turned back to Aiden. "This is the most random team I've ever been on. I have no idea how they put us all together."

"Me either," said Aiden.

"We could be called the Misfits," said Jory. "I've been in this minor hockey association since I was five and never once played with any of these guys. I can't believe I made this team. I think some of these guys just started playing a few years ago."

"Yeah, Mike, the big goalie on the other side, said he just started."

"Tree's in grade seven," said Jory. "I think a few of the other kids are too."

"I'm going to need a list," said Aiden.

"Hey, it'll be on our website. Coach Ira told me that when he called. He said there will be a complete team list with numbers and stuff on it, and that he wants to blog after games. So that's one cool thing. Probably the only cool thing though."

"Yeah," said Aiden. "Let's try and make it good anyway, okay?" Maybe if he kept saying that to everyone, it would happen.

Jory nudged Aiden with his shoulder and cracked a small smile. "Okay. Probably easier said than done, but I'll give it a go."

Aiden was the first one dressed, so when Coach Ira announced that the ice was ready, he was also the first one out of the dressing room.

He stepped on the ice and inhaled a big breath. He took off skating and stretching, doing his regular warm-up routine. He skated around the rink a few times, using his crossovers to get around the corners, then he picked up a puck and skated toward Tree in net. Aiden practised his deke but made sure his shot went to the goalie's pads so he could make the save. His dad had always told him that warm-up meant warming up the goalie too, and that it wasn't just about scoring goals. After a few circles and a few more shots on net, he turned around and practised skating backwards.

Coach Ira blew the whistle for everyone to gather at centre just as Craig stepped on the ice with someone wearing the same track suit as Coach Ira. Craig's frown showed right through his cage; his eyes were slits and his mouth was turned down. Aiden took a quick look around, and at the far end of the arena, he saw Craig's father arguing with someone, his hands waving in the air.

Coach Ira brought Aiden's attention back to the circle, where Craig was now standing behind everyone else. "Team, I would like to introduce my assistant, Coach Ben."

Coach Ben gave a little wave. "Hi, guys."

"First thing we are going to do today," said Coach Ira, "are some simple skating drills, but you will also use a puck at all times. First drill is to skate up and down the ice, pushing the puck forward and keeping your feet moving."

Aiden had to listen carefully, because this wasn't something he'd ever done before. Usually his skating drills were without pucks.

"Okay, so five players will go at a time," said Coach Ira. "Goalies, I want you with Coach Ben for your skating and shooting practice."

Tree and Audrey, another girl from Aiden's school, were the two goalies. Aiden had counted fifteen other players on the team. Three lines of forwards, five players on defence and two goalies. In Florida, every team he had been on had four lines of forwards. Here they said they would pull a player up from the rec team if someone got sick. Three lines meant more ice time in games. Aiden was all for that.

They lined up at the end zone to start the drill, with Aiden in the first group. Coach Ira blew his whistle, and Aiden took off. It was harder with the puck, but Aiden went as fast as he could.

"Heads up!" Coach Ira yelled. "Skate with that puck, but work on keeping your head up."

By the time they got to the other end, the next group was already halfway there.

Aiden had thought skating would be easier with the pucks, but it wasn't. Coach Ira never let them rest. It was bang, bang, get moving, don't stop. He rolled out the lines and kept everyone skating and pushing the puck forward. After ten skates on the first drill, he blew the whistle.

"Now you're going backwards. No pucks for five, then five with pucks."

Ten more times? Aiden's legs were killing him. After the tenth turn, he wanted to drop.

Coach Ira blew the whistle again. "Quick water break, then meet at centre ice!"

Aiden gulped down some water, then headed to the middle of the ice.

"Chop, chop," said Coach Ira. Once everyone was there, he said, "This next drill focuses on skating and footwork, and I'm also putting a 'race' into it for fun. The trick is to keep your feet moving. I want our team to be known as the best skaters. Coach Ben has set up cones for everyone."

Aiden glanced at the orange cones. On either side of centre ice, there were two on the blueline and two along the red line.

"I'm going to split you into two teams, and each team will form a line between the boards and the centre-ice circle. On my whistle, the first player on each team skates forward to the first cone on their team's half of the blueline and goes around it. But here's the deal: you have to get your feet into the offensive zone, otherwise you're disqualified. Coach Ben will be watching. Does everyone understand? This is not just a drill for speed, but also for opening up the hips when skating and pivoting."

Manny put up his hand. "What's the offensive zone?"

"Are you kidding me? You dummy," said Craig.

"Hey, O'Brien, that's not cool," said Coach Ira. "I

asked if there were questions and he had one." He looked directly at Manny. "For now, your offensive zone is the ice past the blueline. But after practice I will explain it to you on the whiteboard, okay?"

"Thanks," said Manny, hanging his head.

"Okay, so once you're over the blueline, pivot and skate backwards to the cone closest to the boards on your team's side of the red line. Then pivot again, go around the cone, and skate forward to the next blueline cone, again getting your feet inside that offensive zone. Then pivot and go backwards again, and skate as fast as you can to the cone located closer to centre ice. It's like a zigzag. Use your edges to get around the cones. Finally, after you go around the last cone, give it what you got and skate to Coach Ben and the pucks on the blueline. Pick up a puck, skate to the net, and shoot. Then head back, and the next player will go. Guys who understand, you go first. Start your line by the boards."

"Such a long explanation for a stupid zigzag," muttered Craig.

They got into their teams, and when the whistle blew, Aiden took off. He gave everything he had to help his team. The backwards skating was killer, but he finished a second ahead of Deke. Next, it was J.J.'s turn. Aiden leaned over his stick to catch his breath. He stood up just as J.J. tried to pivot at the blueline and fell.

"It's okay, J.J., just get up and keep going," Coach Ira called out. "Part of falling is getting up."

J.J. scrambled up.

Both teams were even by the time the last guys had to go, and now it was Jory against Craig. Craig took off and whizzed to the blueline. His pivot was clean and almost rhythmic. Jory struggled a little and tried to catch up, and although he was good on the straightaway, he just couldn't compete.

"Go, Jory," screamed Aiden.

"You can do it!" J.J. screamed.

"Go, B.O.," screamed Manny, who was on the other team.

Aiden glanced over. Had Manny just called Craig B.O.? If he did, Craig hadn't heard. Jory and Craig went backwards, then forward again. Jory had made up a bit of ground on the backwards skating, but Craig got over the blueline first, pivoted again, and took off. Jory made it to the blueline a few seconds later.

Then Coach Ben called out, "Disqualification. Team one didn't touch the offensive zone."

Aiden's team groaned. Jory kept going and finished the drill behind Craig, but Aiden patted his back anyway. "Good try," he said.

"Sucker," said Craig to Jory. "I killed it. Killed you."

"**Shut up**," whispered Jory. Then he turned to

Aiden. "I blew it." He panted, his chest moving up and down.

"It's only the first practice. There's lots of next times," said Aiden.

After another water break, they did more drills. In fact, it was drill after drill after drill, and they were all ones Aiden hadn't done before, so the practice whizzed by. When he finally looked at the clock, there were only ten minutes left.

Coach Ira blew his whistle to get everyone's attention. "I'm going to call out three lines and some defence pairings. I'm hoping I can get a sense of who might work with who by our first game, but it might take a few practices."

Aiden was hoping to get on a line with Jory and Craig. He waited for Coach Ira to call out the names. If he could have crossed his fingers inside his gloves, he would have.

"Okay," said Coach Ira. He pulled his phone out of his pocket and did a quick search. "Got it. Here we go. On the first line is Craig at centre, Jory right wing and J.J. left wing."

Craig slammed his stick against the boards. "I don't want to be with some loser who can't skate!"

"Oh man, this is bad," whispered Jory.

Craig left the group and raced over to the boards

where his dad was watching. He slammed his stick again. Then his dad started shouting at Coach Ira.

"I'll be back in a few seconds," said Coach Ira.

"I'll back you up," said Coach Ben.

The two of them skated over to the boards. Aiden had never seen anything like this at a hockey practice.

"Wow," said Tree. He leaned against his big goalie stick. "This is better than video games."

The entire group stood still and watched the hand waving and shouting. Even though Aiden couldn't hear exactly what they were saying, it was clear how Craig felt. He smacked his stick on the ice again and again. But his dad was even madder, his face super red. He leaned over the boards like he was about to jump onto the ice.

Aiden glanced at J.J., who was hanging his head, then skated over to him.

"Get out there and skate your hardest," said Aiden softly.

"This is all because of me."

"No. He's totally out of line. But you're good at passing, and he's a natural goal scorer. The two of you can do damage. That's the thing about being on a line with someone like him — you can get tons of assists."

J.J. looked at Aiden. "Thanks. I'm so nervous. I've never played with anyone as good as him."

Aiden remembered something his dad had said to

him. "Practice is where you make mistakes. That's why it's called practice."

J.J. nodded. "That makes sense."

Aiden looked back to where Craig was still with his dad and the coaches. Hopefully, they didn't waste all their ice time.

CHAPTER SIX

LINES

Finally Coach Ira skated back over to the group, his face flushed. "I'm sorry you had to see that," he said. His voice seemed a little shaky, but then he took a deep breath and said, "Okay, for the rest of the lines." He got his phone out again and glanced down at it. Then he ran his hand through his hair. "Wow," he said. "I hope everyone else is okay with the lines I made."

"Sure thing, Coach," blurted out Aiden. He felt he had to say something. No one else was.

But then Aiden held his breath. *Who would he be with?* Aiden was disappointed he wasn't on the top line, but maybe Coach Ira was trying to even out the lines? Or maybe he thought J.J. was better than Aiden, that he had more potential? *Maybe he just thought Aiden sucked.* After what Craig had done, Aiden was not going to make a fuss.

"Aiden, Susie and Emmanuel," said Coach Ira.

"Call me Manny," said Manny, in a squeaky voice.

Susie glanced at Aiden and held up her thumb. Aiden did the same back. He liked being with Susie, so this was okay. Aiden tried to get Manny's attention, but he was staring at the stands, looking completely confused by the still-fuming Mr. O'Brien.

"Manny," whispered Aiden.

He turned at the sound of his name.

"We're on a line together."

Manny nodded. "Craig's dad is going *ballistic*."

"Ignore him for now, okay?"

"Okay." Manny saluted. "I'm ready."

"And," said Coach Ira, glancing at his phone again, "Jacob, you're centring a line with Decker and Bilal." Aiden glanced around, realizing Decker was the one everyone had been calling Deke.

Jacob gave Bilal a high-five. Jacob was in seventh grade, and almost as big as Tree. Aiden thought it was interesting that the biggest skater was with the smallest.

"So that's it for the forward lines. Defence, since there's five of you, we will probably be rotating you a lot. Colin and Henry will be together today. Mason, Alvaro and Finn will rotate."

"How are you going to run this drill, Coach?" Craig asked. He'd finally come back to the group. "It makes no sense. We have three lines and five D."

"Good question," said Coach Ira. He turned to Coach Ben and grinned. "You're the math genius. Figure this one out."

"He should have figured this out before practice," muttered Craig.

Coach Ben said, "Pretty basic, Coach. We'll start with two lines on one bench, and one line on the other. I'll time ninety-second shifts. So, two lines will play for ninety seconds, and one will sit. At the end of the shift, one line will stay out and play another shift against the line that was on the bench. Then we'll rotate. Each line will get one long three-minute shift. We'll do the same with D-men. Two on one bench and three on the other, and we'll rotate in the extra player."

"We have to play for three minutes straight?" Manny asked Aiden, as they took their places on the bench. Craig's line was heading out for the first long shift. "Is that what he said?"

"Yeah, but not yet. And only once."

"That's sooooo long. Three minutes will be like an eternity. Like going to space in a capsule and never coming back."

"Dude. Focus," Aiden said, laughing.

Aiden watched from the bench as the scrimmage started. J.J. skated hard up and down the ice, trying to keep up with Craig. Aiden noticed he had long strides; they were just a bit wobbly. Jacob's line batted around the puck, then it got loose and J.J. picked it up. He took a couple of steps, his legs looking like tentacles, but he managed to get off a pass to Craig, who had already pivoted and was heading up the ice. As soon as J.J. released the puck, he fell, sliding headfirst into the boards. But Craig got the puck on his stick anyway and continued racing down the ice.

"Get up, J.J.," called Coach Ira.

J.J. hurried to his feet. Jory skated with Craig to the net, got open, and slapped his stick on the ice. Mason was blocking Craig, and doing a good job of keeping between him and the net. Although Craig could have passed to Jory, who was in the clear, he took the shot himself. Tree made a good save.

Craig smacked his stick on the ice. "You got lucky," he yelled at Tree.

"Yeah, right," said Tree. "No wood on that one."

After another play where Craig didn't pass the puck, Aiden stepped on the ice for his shift. Jory was shaking his head and talking to Craig. "I was wide open," Aiden heard him say.

As the players were getting ready to line up, J.J. skated close to Aiden. "Great passing," said Aiden, as he went by.

J.J. smiled behind his cage. "Thanks!"

Aiden got into position for the faceoff. He looked at Manny on his right and Susie on his left. Behind him, Colin and Henry were on defence.

Aiden curled his bottom hand around the lower end

of his stick. He didn't feel the same nerves he had during tryouts, so he put all his attention on the puck in Coach Ben's hand. He could do this. When Coach Ben dropped the puck, Aiden quickly batted it back to his defence. Colin managed to keep it on his stick and sent it over to Henry. But Craig wheeled in and picked it off, then started skating down the ice on a breakaway. Aiden spun around by opening his hips like they had done in their drills, then dug in his edges and gave chase.

One stride, two strides. He pumped his legs. *Craig was fast. Too fast for him.* But then Mr. O'Brien yelled at Craig from the stands, and he lost his stride for a few steps. Aiden picked up his pace. Quads burning, he got closer. He told himself to just keep skating, pushing and pushing. Now his quads were screaming, but he kept his legs moving. At the blueline, he was close. Was the puck within reach? Aiden poked it with his stick, and suddenly it was loose. Aiden made a quick turn, picked up the puck, and spotted Susie on the wing. He made a tape-to-tape pass just as Craig pushed Aiden to the ice. Susie sailed over the red line anyway. She rushed forward, pushing by Finn on defence.

As he was scrambling up, Aiden saw Manny on his other side. "Go to the net!" Aiden yelled to him.

Manny crashed toward the net just as Susie rifled off a shot. The puck hit his knee, then popped past Audrey and into the net.

"Did I just score?" Manny asked.

Aiden laughed and patted his back. "You sure did."

"Wow. I never score." Manny slid to the ice and did a victory cheer.

"Um, it is just a scrimmage" said Susie, who was also laughing.

Coach Ira lifted the side of his mouth in a little smile, shook his head, and said, "Okay, let's keep the scrimmage going. Save the dramatics for your first goal during a game." Then he skated over to Aiden. "Where did those wheels come from?" He laughed. "That was a good backcheck. Good hustle. O'Brien's a fast skater."

Craig skated by Aiden. "I let you catch me," he said. "Just to see what you're made of."

"Yeah, right," said Aiden. *Why hadn't he skated like that in tryouts?*

When the scrimmage was over, Aiden went to the dressing room exhausted. His legs felt like jelly.

"That was a hard practice," said Jory, as he tossed his shoulder pads into his hockey bag. "No breaks at all." He wiped sweat off his face with a towel.

"Yeah, I thought so too," said Aiden. He leaned back against the wall. "I really liked it though. We did some stuff I've never done before."

"Yeah, me too," said Jory. "Nice not to do the same old, same old."

"Oh, I thought it was just me," said Aiden. "Because I haven't played here before."

Jory shook his head. "Last year we did the same things over and over. This was good today. Coach Ira is pretty creative. Some of those drills were super hard, but I liked them all. Plus, we kept moving the entire practice. I hate it when you stand around. That three-minute shift was a killer though."

The chatter around the room grew as guys undressed. Everyone was almost changed and in street clothes when Coach Ira came in. "Is everyone decent?" he asked. He glanced around. "I'm going to get Susie and Audrey in here. Don't leave, okay?"

"My dad is waiting for me," said Craig. "I have to go."

"I'll talk to your dad," said Coach Ira. "I need you to stay."

Craig shook his head as if this was a huge inconvenience for him. As soon as Coach Ira left, Craig started mimicking him. "I'll talk to your dad. You're not allowed to leave." He rolled his eyes. "Our coach blows."

"I thought he was good," said Manny. "I've never been so tired in my whole life."

Craig glared at him. "That's because you're out of shape, Doughboy."

Manny hung his head. "Sorry, B.O."

"What did you call me?" Craig squirted water in Manny's face.

"Uh-oh," said Jory. He started laughing. Then he whispered to Aiden, "No one calls him B.O."

"Isn't that your hockey nickname?" Manny looked genuinely confused. "I know kids at school just call you O'Brien, but I thought your hockey nickname was B.O."

"You dingbat. Don't you ever call me that again," said Craig. Then he stood up. "And that goes for everyone in here." He threw a roll of tape at Manny, and it hit him in the shoulder.

"Why'd you do that?" Manny asked.

Aiden heard J.J. whisper to Manny, "It's O.B., not B.O. B.O. means you stink. Like body odour."

"I know *that*," said Manny. "I thought it was an inside joke."

Fortunately, Coach Ira banged the door open, and everyone's attention turned to him, Susie and Audrey.

"That was a great practice, team," said Coach Ira. If he felt the tension in the room, he was good at hiding it.

"I'm pretty pumped," he continued, without missing a beat. "And I know we are going to keep getting better. Since this is our first practice, we need to go over a few things. First off, we will need to pick captains."

Aiden glanced over at Craig. Would he end up being the captain because he was the best player? Aiden swore that Craig puffed out his chest a little, sat taller and smirked more. Aiden sighed. Poor Manny.

"Us coaches will pick the captain, and you will all vote for alternate captains. We will have two. One will wear the 'A' at home, and the other will wear the 'A' at away games. That will all happen on Saturday." He paused and looked at his phone.

"We will also need to pick a name for our team so we can cheer before games!"

"Who cares about cheering. We're not five," muttered Craig.

Coach Ira ignored him. "I would like everyone to submit a team name on Saturday. I will read them aloud and then we will take a vote to decide which one is the best."

There were a few whispers from the group, but Coach Ira put up his hand. "We only have a few more practices before our first game. I will be looking to put lines together during those practices, but as you can see from today, I'm also going to be working on skills — and that means individual skills. At each practice, I'll increase the tempo, and we'll flow from one drill to the next. Be prepared to skate."

He paused, looked around at everyone, and smiled. "But we're going to have some fun too. First pizza party will also be Saturday, after practice and a parents' meeting.

I've booked the room upstairs. Yes, your parents will be invited to eat pizza too. We have a big surprise we want to announce that day. It's something exciting for the organization, and everyone is super stoked about it."

"Tell us now, Coach!" Tree yelled.

Coach Ira grinned. "You have to wait."

"Come on, Coach," said Jory. "You can't leave us hanging."

"Saturday! I promise. It could end up being a big deal in the future too. You will get to grow up and say you were part of the first one ever!"

"No fair," said Manny. "But I love surprises."

Aiden was pretty sure he knew what the big surprise was. He figured Craig did too, because he rolled his eyes and muttered, "Whatever. It's so stupid anyway."

Something heavy settled in Aiden's stomach. *Everyone at the tournament would be watching him, judging him.*

Coach Ira held up his hand again. "Now, moving on, let's have a drum roll please."

Everyone in the room started tapping their legs.

Then Coach Ira said, "We won the lottery for extra ice time! Our next practice is Thursday morning at six a.m."

Manny groaned.

"No moaning allowed," said Coach Ira. "Every team wanted this extra ice, and if I'm getting up that early, so are you."

CHAPTER SEVEN

GRANDPA'S ADVICE

On his way out of the dressing room, Aiden ran into Ned.

"That was some practice," Ned said, as he patted Aiden's back. He was grinning from ear to ear. "I like that coach you got. He runs . . . a practice and a half. Good use of ice time."

Aiden tilted his head and looked at Ned's weathered face. Ned knew a lot more than anyone gave him credit for. He'd been working at this arena for years, and he saw everything that happened inside it.

"Yeah," said Aiden. "I liked his drills."

Ned took his Florida Panthers ball cap off, scratched his head, and put his hat back on. "You got a . . . problem kid though."

"He'll probably be our captain."

"Your daddy was always captain," Ned said, then nodded. "I bet he . . . taught you a few things."

"I've never been a captain," said Aiden. "Not even an alternate." He paused. He didn't usually want to talk about his dad, but it seemed okay with Ned. He didn't have that same curiosity about what had happened and just wanted to talk about his dad as a player. "Um, what was my dad like as a captain?"

"Oh boy," said Ned. "Could he get a team fired up on the . . . bench. To him every line was important too. And no matter what, even if a goal went in, he talked to his goalie."

"What else do you remember about him?"

"Oh, lots and lots."

Aiden desperately wanted to hear more about his father. Ned could tell him. Aiden looked at Ned, then he whispered, "Are we still going on the ice? We could go tomorrow morning."

Ned shrugged. "I dunno. Arena's closed tomorrow."

"Please, Ned? You could help me and tell me more about my dad," Aiden said quietly.

Ned held his finger up to his mouth. Then he leaned into Aiden and whispered, "Tomorrow at six a.m. Thirty . . . minutes. No more."

"I'll be there," said Aiden.

Ned patted Aiden's back. "I want to show you something your daddy gave me."

"What is it?"

Ned waggled his finger. "Has to be a surprise."

Aiden laughed. "Sounds like a plan, man. Look, I better go. See you tomorrow."

When he got to the lobby, all of Aiden's teammates were gone and his mother was waiting for him. "Where have you been? You've been off the ice for forty minutes," she said.

"Talking to Ned."

Aiden's mom smiled and put her arm around him. "Ned's been a fixture at this arena for as long as I can remember." She gave his shoulder a squeeze. "Now we better get going. Grandpa will want to eat. It's late for him."

* * *

"How was your practice?" Grandpa asked at dinner. Aiden almost fell off his chair. He glanced at his mother, and she looked as shocked as he felt. Since they had moved to Prairie Field, Grandpa had been quiet and didn't talk much. Aiden's mom said having them move in was an adjustment for him too. But they'd had to because his memory wasn't great.

"It was great, Grandpa," said Aiden. "We have this really young coach, but he did some cool drills that I've never done before."

"That's good. Young players need to be challenged. I used to read playbooks to come up with new drills."

Aiden hadn't ever really talked to his grandpa about how he had coached. Aiden's dad had talked about Grandpa a lot though, and in every magazine interview or speech, or whenever someone asked about who had inspired his hockey, he always mentioned Grandpa and thanked him for being his best minor hockey coach and for basically saving him, encouraging him and helping him make the NHL.

"I think that's what my coach is doing too." Aiden paused for a moment, and since Grandpa still looked interested, he said, "They're going to name the captains soon. The coach is picking the captain, and we're voting on the alternates."

Grandpa nodded. "Being a captain is not just about being popular." He looked up and stared Aiden in the eyes. "Don't just vote for the player who is the best. They can be the cocky ones."

"Okay," said Aiden. He liked this side of Grandpa. "Any other tips you can give me, Grandpa?"

Aiden's grandpa sat back in his chair. He crossed his arms and looked to the ceiling.

"Hmmm," he said. "A captain has to pull everyone together. Teams win because they have some fun in the dressing room and work hard on the ice." He looked straight ahead. "A captain is someone who leads both on and off the ice."

"Wow, Dad," said Aiden's mom. "You're really giving Aiden some good advice."

"Aiden?" Grandpa squinted at Aiden. "Aren't you Luke?"

"Aiden is my son, Dad. And I'm your daughter. So, he's your grandson."

"Oh, is that so," said Grandpa. He waved his hand. "I knew that."

Whether he did or didn't, Aiden liked talking to him about hockey. "Any more advice you can give me, Grandpa?" Aiden asked.

"Do your school work." Then Grandpa looked away, staring out the window.

"Okay." Aiden glanced at his mother, and she shrugged. He guessed the conversation was probably over.

"You done, Dad?" Aiden's mom stood up and started clearing the table. Aiden got up to help her.

"I'm going to the living room," said Grandpa. His hands shook as he put them on the table to push himself up.

Instead of picking up plates, Aiden moved over beside his grandfather and got his cane so he could safely move from the table to the sofa in the living room. "There you go, Grandpa," he said, handing it to him. Then he held out his hands. "Let me help you up."

"You're a good kid," said Grandpa.

"Thanks," said Aiden. "And you're a good grandpa. Thanks for the advice."

"What advice?"

"The hockey advice."

"Oh, that. Make sure you put in extra practice. Do your homework." Then he walked out of the room. Aiden couldn't help but stare after him. That conversation had been sort of surreal.

When Grandpa was safely sitting on the sofa, Aiden helped his mother put the dishes in the dishwasher.

"It was good advice he gave me," Aiden said to his mother.

Aiden had been tossing around voting for Craig as one of the alternates, but now he didn't think that was such a good idea. *What if Coach Ira made Craig the captain?* That could be disastrous. *He was so much better than every player on the team.* But Grandpa just said it wasn't always the best player who made the best captain. Thoughts swirled through Aiden's mind. As for alternates, Aiden thought Jory would be good. But who else?

"It sure was," said his mother. She glanced over at him. "You seem like you're in a better mood."

"Tryouts are over. That's kind of a relief, since I didn't play very well." Aiden looked away. No way was he telling her he kept seeing Dad's face. "Now there's not much I can do but try to get better so I can make a good team next year. So . . . it is what it is. And I really want to play well in this tournament."

"That's the attitude. I know you're under more

scrutiny here because of your dad, and that can be hard and nerve-racking," said his mother. "I think you're handling this so well." Aiden's mom looked at him and smiled. She gently snapped a drying towel at him. "I can do these dishes. You should do your homework."

"I need to use my iPad," he said. "To do some research." That was partly true, but what Aiden was researching was his team's website.

"Sure," said Aiden's mother, "but you know the rule. Devices off at nine o'clock and down here to charge."

"Got it," said Aiden.

Aiden hesitated for a minute. He was going to tell his mother that he was going on the ice with Ned in the morning, but for some reason the words wouldn't come out. *What if she said no?* His dad had done it, so why couldn't he? He wanted to be able to shoot like his dad had. And Grandpa *did* say to put in extra practice.

No, he wouldn't tell her.

He wouldn't tell anyone.

CHAPTER EIGHT

EARLY MORNINGS

The alarm on Aiden's phone went off at five thirty on Wednesday morning, and Aiden quickly reached over to silence it. He lay still and listened to the old house creak. Sometimes Aiden would hear Grandpa up in the night, roaming around downstairs in the dark. But this morning everything was quiet.

The tricky part of getting out of the house was creeping down the stairs without them groaning. One step. Two steps. Aiden tiptoed down each stair until he hit the landing. Darkness oozed through the house, but he didn't dare turn a light on.

His hockey skates, stick and helmet sat strategically at the back door. Aiden had even been smart enough to tuck a granola bar and orange juice container into his helmet so he could have something to eat. The back door squeaked as he stepped outside. Aiden closed it softly behind him and sucked in a deep breath of fresh morning air. Talk about cold! The mornings were getting colder and colder every day, and now a layer of frost covered the brown grass.

Once his eyes had adjusted to the lack of light, Aiden slung his skates over his shoulder and ran to the arena with them slapping against his side. Five minutes later he arrived, and Ned ushered him in, locking the door behind them.

"This is kind of spooky," said Aiden. Only the emergency lights were glowing inside the arena.

"That is just what your daddy said too. Get your skates on, and I'll turn on a few lights. No lobby or outside ones though."

Aiden was sitting on the players' bench tying his skates when the buzz of the lights being switched on echoed through the arena. *What if someone saw the lights? Would they be in trouble?*

Aiden couldn't think about that right now. He needed to focus on getting better, improving — just like his dad. He stepped on the ice and tossed a couple of pucks down. Something surged inside him. It was just him on the ice, skating all alone, his edges digging in and making crunching sounds. He went side to side on his skates just to hear the sound echo. Then he picked up a puck, put it on the end of his stick, and skated around, stickhandling to the end of the ice and back. The arena was so quiet that the clunk of the puck hitting the boards bounced against the arena walls. Aiden exhaled and felt his body relax in a way it hadn't since he'd arrived in Prairie Field. He smiled behind his cage.

The gate clanged, and Aiden turned to see Ned stepping on the ice in full gear. Aiden grinned. Ned looked so retro! Like a goalie from the old days. Johnny Bower old. Ken Dryden old. Grandpa's heroes. His pads were made of old brown leather, and they were so small — nothing like today's goalie pads. But he also wore a modern goaltending helmet.

"Looking good, Ned. Where'd you get the Panthers mask?"

"That's what I wanted to show you," he said. "That's the surprise. Your daddy brought it back for me one summer."

He skated over, and Aiden was impressed. Ned had good balance and edge control. Someone taught him well. Maybe even Grandpa.

"He said I deserved it for being his . . . target practice all those years. Pretty special," Ned said, then pointed to the nets off to the side. "We'll need one of those."

"On it," said Aiden. He skated over to the edge of the ice, stepped onto the rubber matting, and pulled one of the nets onto the ice. Then he pushed it into place.

"Okay," said Ned. "Wrist shot first."

Ned made Aiden shoot from all different angles. Much to Aiden's surprise, Ned stopped a lot of his shots — way more than half. Then Ned had Aiden pretend he was at target practice. He wanted Aiden to rapid fire shot after shot after shot. Sweat started to drip down Aiden's back. Ned moved in and out of the net, trying to stop Aiden's shots. Some went in, lots were batted out by Ned and too many missed the net entirely.

"Keep firing," said Ned.

Aiden shook out his arms, then shot a few more times.

"Okay, now for the fun," said Ned. "Let's work on some dekes."

Time after time, Ned wanted Aiden to shoot from his backhand on the deke, which was Aiden's weakest shot.

"That's why you got to work on that one," Ned said, when Aiden protested. "I watched ya. I know what you need to do. Release quicker. Don't . . . hesitate."

Aiden's arms were killing him by the time the thirty minutes were up. "That was great, Ned," said Aiden. "Thanks. I might not be able to write at school today, but I bet I can shoot better at the next practice."

"Just like your daddy. Always saying thank you. Always willing to work. I need to get out of this gear," said Ned, "and get the . . . lights off."

"Do you think it's okay we're here?" Aiden asked. His heart did a few fast beats. He had convinced himself it was all fine, but . . . was it really?

Ned shrugged. "We didn't turn on any outside lights. And it was only thirty . . . minutes."

"That's true. I'll take care of the net, then I'm gonna run home," said Aiden. He held up his fist, and Ned bumped it.

Aiden raced home in the still-dark morning, his skates swinging. When he got back to his house, all the lights were still off and he breathed a sigh of relief. Now, to get in and get back up to bed. He snuck in and carefully put his skates on the floor. Then he slipped off his shoes and tiptoed through the kitchen toward the stairs. He crept upstairs without waking anyone. When he made to his room, he plopped down on his bed. It was now six forty. He could go back to sleep for at least half an hour.

Aiden was in a deep sleep when his mother woke him up by shaking his shoulders. "Aiden! Come on, get up. I've called you three times now."

He rolled over and shook his head. His mom was standing over him. "Why are you wearing your track suit?" She frowned at him.

"Um, it was freezing in here last night."

She sighed. "I'll try and get this furnace fixed. Always something to do in this house." She walked toward the door. "I'll meet you downstairs for breakfast. I'm working at the gift store today." Aiden's mother was technically a nurse, but since she had to take care of Grandpa, she just worked in a gift store a few days a week to get out of the house.

Like a zombie, Aiden got dressed for school, ate breakfast, brushed his teeth, and got on the bus. He sat in the first available seat he saw and was dozing off when someone sat down beside him, the seat cushion squeaking with the pressure. Aiden opened one eye.

"How come you're sitting at the front?" Jory asked.

"I'm tired," said Aiden.

Jory leaned into Aiden. "Who you voting for?" he whispered.

Aiden took a quick glance around the bus.

"Don't worry, he's at the back."

"Do you think Craig will be captain?" Aiden asked.

"I hope not. But then I kind of hope he will. My brain goes back and forth, like a ball in a tennis match." Jory slapped his head. "I just want to have a good year, and either way isn't going to be good. If he's not captain, he'll be a pain, and if he is captain, he'll be mean. I wish he'd get moved up."

"Any word on that?" Aiden asked.

"Not that I've heard. Have you heard anything? I think his dad has been barking like a mad dog, ordering the president of our minor hockey association to have meetings with him. I heard he even went over and whaled on Mr. Ramos's door, like, with his fist. Just pounded on it. It's nuts."

"I hope Mr. O'Brien doesn't show up at practice tomorrow. I felt sorry for our coaches last practice."

"Me too," said Jory. "Glad we got the ice though. It's just so early."

"Yeah," said Aiden. Then he leaned his head against the window. "Soooo early."

"Early or not, we're lucky we got it. Otherwise we might have to drive over an hour to another arena for extra practice. And on this team, I'm not sure a lot of the parents will pay to get ice time elsewhere. That will make Mr. O'Brien go ballistic. He's still mad about the vote they had last spring, on whether to close the arena part time or raise the fees. Craig said he thought everyone should just pay the extra fees. But so many people don't have jobs because of oil and gas being so bad."

Aiden slouched farther down his seat. Now he knew he couldn't say anything to anyone about being in the arena with Ned.

* * *

"I'm jacked to the roof for practice tomorrow morning," Susie said to Aiden in science. They'd done such a good job on their last lab that they had been teamed up again to work on a solar-system project. Susie was strategically drawing the planets on a big piece of white paper, and

Aiden was writing down the notes. She was way better at drawing than Aiden was. In fact, her drawings were amazing. Aiden was impressed.

"It'll be early." Aiden yawned. His shooting practice with Ned was already catching up to him.

"Yes, but just think how *invigorated* we will feel all day at school."

Aiden glanced at her. "Seriously?" he said. "Invigorated? Are you like a battery that never runs out of power? I might be pressing the snooze button all day tomorrow."

"Don't forget we have to hand in our English outline tomorrow too. What are you doing your essay on?"

"I dunno." Aiden shrugged, then changed the subject. "What planet am I researching again?"

"Mercury," she said. "I'm doing my story on my brother. He has autism."

"Sorry to hear that."

She shook her head at Aiden. "Don't be sorry. That's who he is."

Aiden thought about Ned. He was who he was too. He might have his quirks and be slow at some things because of his brain injury, but he was fast at others. And he sure knew hockey. Just look at how he had helped Aiden that morning.

"So," Susie said. "You never answered. What are *you* writing about?"

"I dunno. The difference between hockey here and in Florida?"

"Um, not to burst your bubble or anything, but Mr. Rowland said no hockey stories. Maybe that could be okay if you added personal stuff in there. I mean, look at all you could write about. How people react to hockey in different countries and the tryouts and moving and . . . that's three paragraphs right there. But if I were you, I'd talk to Mr. Rowland first. He might not like the topic and then you'd waste your time doing an outline. If I was the teacher, I would allow it."

"You're not the teacher though."

Susie stopped working on her drawings and glanced over at Aiden.

"What?" he asked. *Why was she was staring at him?*

"I live with my mother too," she said. "Just for the record."

"So?" Aiden looked down. He could feel his throat starting to clog and his body heat up. *He didn't want to talk about his dad in this classroom!* Not after what had been said behind his back.

"What I'm saying is I don't have a dad either."

"Oh. I'm sorry."

"But he didn't die like your dad did." She looked down at her drawing.

What was that supposed to mean? No one died like his dad did.

"He left and we haven't seen him in a long time," continued Susie. "So, it's me and my brother and my mother, and I have to do a lot of stuff to help out. Like, a lot. Sometimes it's *exhausting.*"

"You get exhausted? That's hard to believe."

She playfully punched his arm. "Yes. Sometimes I do get tired, like when I have to cook dinner. I hate that job, and I suck at it. Yesterday I made Kraft Dinner, and it was gross because I added the milk before draining the water." She slapped her forehead. "My brother called it KD soup! It was *dis-gusting.* Even the pigs wouldn't eat it. I'm putting some of that in my story, but also some stuff about how I miss my dad."

"Sorry about your dad." Aiden didn't want to talk about dads anymore, so he asked, "You have pigs?"

She frowned at him. "You already said sorry. I'm sorry about your dad too. I read what happened. The whole story. And, yes, we have two pet pigs."

Aiden nodded and looked back down at his paper. She read about what happened to his dad? *Which story? The not-true one they blew up or the real story?*

"It's cool you have pet pigs," he said. "What are their names?"

"Sid and Hay, after Sidney Crosby and Hayley Wickenheiser."

"Cool. Um, did you say Mercury?" he asked.

"Hey, don't go weird on me. I know some of what they said was lies."

Aiden didn't look up. Susie's father might have left, but he might come back. Aiden's father was never coming back, and it hurt way too much to write about him — or talk about what had happened.

CHAPTER NINE

WEIRDEST PRACTICE EVER

When Aiden's alarm went off the next morning, he groaned out loud. An early morning two days in a row was Killer with a capital K, but as much as getting up early sucked, practising didn't. While he was struggling to get into his old sweatpants, he heard the knock on his door.

"Aiden?" said his mom.

"I'm up," he grumbled.

The door slowly opened, and she stood in his door frame wearing her coral-coloured robe.

"Please, tell me you're driving me," Aiden said.

"Yes," she said, "and I've got some breakfast ready for you."

She looked as tired as he felt. Sometimes he heard her up in the night too. She said she didn't sleep well but that's because she got up to cry.

"Thanks, Mom. I'll be down in a second."

Aiden's mother didn't even get dressed to take him over to the arena, she just threw a coat over her robe. She pulled up to the front doors and popped the trunk. "I'll go back home, get dressed, and come pick you up. Have a good practice."

"Sounds good," said Aiden. At least in Prairie Field everything was close by.

On his way into the arena, Aiden ran into Coach Ira. His hair was frizzing out all over the place, and his eyes were slivers, like they should be closed instead of open. Coach Ben was sitting on the bench in the lobby with his hat pulled over his eyes.

"Hi Aiden," said Coach Ira, his voice gravelly. "Room three."

"Thanks," Aiden mumbled back. There was no high-fiving or fist bumping this morning.

Once again, Aiden was the first one in the dressing room, and he was getting suited up when the guys trickled in. No one talked very much, just the odd mumble. When it was time to go on the ice, Aiden took a head count. Everyone had shown up except for Manny.

"J.J.," said Aiden, as they were skating and stretching to warm up, "where's Manny?"

J.J. shrugged. "I don't know. He said he was coming."

Aiden tapped J.J. on the shins with his stick. "Let's have a good practice," he said. Then Aiden took off skating, using long strides to stretch out his legs.

As Aiden rounded the corner, he saw Mr. O'Brien, skates on, stepping on the ice. Uh-oh. Coach Ira skated over to Mr. O'Brien, and Aiden slowed down to listen to their conversation.

"I already have my assistant on the ice with me," Coach Ira said.

"You're a couple of kids," replied Mr. O'Brien. "Neither of you knows a thing about coaching."

"Any parent going on the ice has to be cleared by the association," said Coach Ira.

"It'll be fine. I'll talk to Ramos later. I'm on the ice today and I'm helping you run this practice. If my kid has to play for you, I'm at least going to see to it that he gets a good practice in. These boys need to skate."

"Boys and girls. There's two on the team."

"And that's a joke too."

"This is brutal," Jory said to Aiden. Aiden hadn't even heard Jory skate up to him. How could Mr. O'Brien say that about Susie? Next to Craig, Susie was the best skater on the team.

"Mr. O'Brien's never done this before. Ever," said Jory.

"He's acting like a jerk," said Aiden. Aiden looked over at Craig. As much as Craig wasn't his favourite person, it was kind of awful seeing him with his head hanging and his shoulders so slumped.

"I'd be so ticked at my dad," said Jory.

"Come on," said Aiden. "Let's go over to him."

"Why?" Jory asked.

"Because he's our teammate," said Aiden.

Aiden and Jory skated over to Craig. "Hey, O.B.," Aiden said.

"What do you want?" Craig snarled like a mean raccoon.

"Let's have a good practice," said Aiden.

"As if," said Craig. "My dad is such a jerk. Why does he have to ruin everything?"

The whistle blew, and Aiden quickly skated to the faceoff circle and got down on one knee. His father had always told him to be in the front row, and to listen to the coach from a kneeling position. The rest of the team followed Aiden's lead and also knelt — even Craig. Coach Ira looked down at Aiden for a brief second. Aiden knew he was stressed, big time, by the way he kept scratching his thigh with his fingers. That was something Aiden did too. It didn't help that Mr. O'Brien was standing at the back of the circle, watching.

Coach Ira had brought a whiteboard with him today and gave it to Coach Ben to hold while he talked.

"Okay, the first drill," said Coach Ira. His voice sounded a bit shaky. "We are going to skate with the pucks again. Same drill as last time for the first few minutes, then I want you to skate around the cones." He pointed to a diagram on the whiteboard. "This is where they will be located."

Mr. O'Brien piped up from the back. "Son, they need to be bag skated."

"That's not what I have planned. Not this morning," said Coach Ira. Aiden noticed the squeaky voice again.

"I've been at this game a long time," said Mr. O'Brien. "I know what I'm talking about."

"I understand," said Coach Ira, "but—"

"Everyone line up at the end zone." Mr. O'Brien waved his stick in the air. "We'll bag skate, then we'll do those other fancy-dancy drills."

Players slowly got up, but no one moved to the end zone.

Coach Ira shook his head. "I'm running this practice."

"You talking back to me? I'm the adult here." Mr. O'Brien pointed to himself. "Me. I've got years of experience on you. If you were half the coach you think you are, you'd want to learn from me."

"Unbelievable," whispered Tree. "This is better than WWE, except it's real! Well, and no punches. Yet, anyway."

Coach Ira's face was crimson, his cheeks splotchy. Aiden glanced around at his teammates. They were just standing like statues, staring at Mr. O'Brien. The whole situation was unbelievably awkward.

"I said, get to the end zone!" Mr. O'Brien pointed

the tip of his stick to where he wanted everyone to go.

Aiden heard grumbling. Then some players started moving as if they thought they should listen to Mr. O'Brien. Aiden stayed by Coach Ira.

"Craig! You're going to be the captain of this team." Mr. O'Brien's voice was even louder now. "You need to tell them what to do."

"Let's go, guys," said Craig. "Time to skate."

About half of the players followed Craig to the end zone. Aiden stared at Coach Ira and said, "I'll stay with you, Coach."

"It's okay, Aiden. Go skate." Coach Ira blew out a rush of air and ran his hand through his hair. "I'll deal with this later. I want you to at least get a practice in, and me fighting with him will just eat up our ice time."

Aiden finally stood up. "You sure?"

"Positive."

Aiden was the last of the team to join everyone on the end-zone line. Coach Ira skated over and stood beside Mr. O'Brien, who had a look of smug satisfaction on his face.

"I'll take it from here," said Coach Ira.

"Sure. But here's what they'll do." Mr. O'Brien rambled off instructions for the classic blue-line-drop, red-line-drop-and-roll, blue-line-dive drill. It was nothing new, so everyone understood. Mr. O'Brien told Coach Ira to blow the whistle.

For the next twenty minutes, Aiden skated. Hard. Mr. O'Brien's drills were nothing creative, but they were tiring.

"This is boring," Jory said to Aiden, as they were waiting their turn.

"At least it's skating," said Aiden.

"Yeah, guess so. I would hate to be O.B. right now."

"Yeah, me too."

Craig had been winning most of the skating races, but his dad still kept screaming at him to go faster.

After they skated Mr. O'Brien's drills, Coach Ira managed to fit in some of the drills he had tried to explain on the whiteboard. Mr. O'Brien spent the rest of his time skating beside Craig and hollering at him if he missed a pass or got the puck tangled in his skates, which fortunately for Craig, didn't happen all that often.

After practice was over, it was a rush to get out of the dressing room. Everyone's parents were waiting to pick them up and get to school on time. Aiden hopped in the front seat of the car. His mom was now dressed in black tights and a knee-length sweater thing that wrapped around her.

"How was practice?" she asked, as she glanced in her side mirror and pulled away from the curb.

"Awkward. Mr. O'Brien came on the ice in his skates. He bossed Coach Ira around and changed up his practice plan."

Aiden's mother took her gaze off the road to look at Aiden. Her eyes were wide. "You're kidding, right?"

Aiden shook his head. "Wish I was. It was *the worst*."

"That's disgusting," she said. "He hasn't changed a bit. He used to play with your dad, you know."

"Really? What was he like back then? I can't imagine."

"In juniors he was always saying things to the guys who weren't as good as he was. He treated the fourth line horribly. Your dad was captain and spent more time dealing with him than anyone on the team. It was like he was toxic in the dressing room. That's what your dad always said."

"Toxic," said Aiden. "That's a good word. Craig is toxic in our dressing room."

"Len, that's Mr. O'Brien, wanted to be in the NHL. He kept trying and even went to some training camps, but when he got cut from a team and sent down to the minors, he'd blame it on everyone but himself."

"He was mean to Craig today. I kinda felt sorry for him."

"I should say something," she said, as she stopped at a stop sign.

"I don't think that's a good idea, Mom. Maybe

Coach Ira will figure this out." Aiden didn't want his mother involved at all.

"What was that man thinking?" His mom sounded mad. "Craig is his own son, and Ira is a high-school student. It is so unfair for an adult to do something like this."

"Got that right," said Aiden. "But promise me you won't say anything. You have to promise."

She sighed. "Okay, but you let me know if you need my help in any way. I mean that — in any way."

"Will do."

* * *

Aiden pulled his coat collar up as he walked into the schoolyard. The day was bright, but there was a cool breeze in the air. It would probably snow again soon. Aiden had heard them talking about it on the weather channel that Grandpa watched ad nauseam, which made no sense to Aiden because Grandpa hardly went outside.

Aiden was walking quickly, his head down, when he heard his name. He turned to see Manny trotting toward him.

"Wait up," Manny called, waving his arms furiously.

Aiden slowed down. "Where were you this morning?" he asked, once Manny was beside him.

"I didn't have a ride." Manny tried to catch his breath. "I got up . . . but my mom wouldn't drive me . . ." He sucked in a deep breath, then exhaled before he said, "She said it was too early and she can't leave my younger brothers and sisters alone. My dad's away again."

Aiden thought about what his mother had said about helping. She was the one who offered her services to help in *any* way. This was a way. "My mom and I will pick you up next time," said Aiden.

"Really? Oh, wow, that'd be great. Was it a good practice?"

"It was . . . different." Aiden saw Mr. Rowland standing at the door with his arms crossed.

"Did Coach tell you what the surprise was?"

"No, not yet."

"I heard it was a big tournament. Like, huge. So they can raise money for the lights."

"Who'd you hear that from?"

"I heard a couple of adults talking about it in the hallway," said Manny. "I think they're doing all kinds of things to make money too. Like T-shirts and stuff."

T-shirts? Would his dad's name and face be on them? Terrific.

CHAPTER TEN

VOTING FOR CAPTAINS

"Outlines for your personal essay need to be on my desk before the end of the day," said Mr. Rowland, after morning announcements.

Aiden had totally forgotten about his outline until late the night before. He'd spent hours on the team website, then when he'd remembered his homework, he'd whipped off a couple of lines about hockey in Florida versus hockey here. His three points had been: 1) It was warm in Florida and you could go to the arena in shorts year-round; 2) There were more teams here; 3) In Florida hardly anyone at school played hockey and here almost everyone did.

After that morning's practice, he felt like he could write an entirely new outline about how parents in Canada were one hundred percent — no, more like five hundred percent — more intense than the parents in Florida. He could add that *personally* it had made him super uncomfortable to have a father get on the ice, talk down to the coaches, and yell at his own son.

At recess, Aiden was standing by himself, feeling

awkward and boring once again, when Manny came up to him.

"J.J. told me what happened this morning. Sounds disastrous."

Aiden was thankful for someone to talk to, so he said, "Yeah, for sure. It was pretty weird." Craig hadn't shown up for school that morning either. Maybe he'd faked being sick? If Aiden's dad had ever done that, Aiden for sure would have faked sick to save face.

"Craig's nasty too, like his dad," said Manny. "I think that's where he gets it from. He's been mean since like grade two. He used to throw stones at me. I'm always glad when he's not at school."

"Stones?" said Aiden. "Are you serious?"

"Rocks too. One time I had a huge bruise. I lied to my mom about it. When he was being mean to me, my mom would say that kids who are bullies are sometimes bullied by someone else. They have to learn it somewhere." He paused and shrugged. "What'd you write your paper on?"

"Um, hockey in Florida compared to here. What about you?"

"Being bullied."

"That sucks," said Aiden. "I'm sorry he did that to you."

"It's not your fault." Manny smiled at Aiden. "You're not the one doing the bullying. You're actually really nice."

* * *

At the end of the day, Aiden put his brief outline on top of the pile on Mr. Rowland's desk. Once it was out of his hands, he scooted out of the classroom, grabbed his coat, and headed to the front entrance instead of the bus. His mom was picking him up because they were going shopping, but all Aiden wanted to do was go home and have a nap.

"You're not catching the bus either?" Jory's voice almost woke Aiden from a standing sleep.

"Nah. Gotta get groceries with my mom. If I don't go, there won't be any good snacks."

"I hear you. I've got a dentist appointment." Jory paused. "That was horrible this morning. I talked to my dad, and he thought Coach Ira handled himself okay. He wanted to say something, but I said not to, like no way."

"My mom wanted to say something too, and I told her Coach Ira could handle it. Have you talked to O'Brien at all?"

"Nope. I was going to at school, but he never showed. His dad probably let him sleep in because he thinks he needs rest for hockey more than he needs to go to school."

"You're kidding me. Lucky. I wish my mom would do that."

"Yeah, me too," said Jory. "Once I told my parents that Craig got to stay home, and they basically told me that would never happen in a million years."

"My grandpa always talks about how important school is. Well, when he can remember."

"I heard your grandpa was one of the best minor hockey coaches Prairie Field ever had. Maybe you can convince him to come out to one of our practices?"

Aiden laughed. "Don't think *that's* going to happen." Just then his mother pulled up with his grandpa in the front seat. "See that old guy? That's my grandpa. I don't think he's up for putting on skates."

Jory laughed, and when Aiden's grandpa waved, Jory waved back as if he knew him. "See ya," said Jory. "Oh, and let's text later about Saturday. You know, the captain vote. I have an idea."

Aiden held up his hand. "Later."

As Aiden got in the back seat, his mother turned and smiled at him. "Who was that?"

"A kid from my team. Jory." Aiden wondered what Jory's idea was.

"Why don't you invite him over sometime? I could make pizzas and popcorn and . . . you know what *eeeelse*." She smiled as she sang the last word.

In Florida, Aiden's house had been the go-to hang-out spot. His hockey team was always around, and they swam, played basketball in the pool and mini sticks in the garage. His mom made food — so much food. The guys loved her sundae bars with ice cream and candy and sprinkles and whipped cream. They would talk about the sundaes for days after.

"Okay," said Aiden. "I guess I could." The heavy feeling returned to the pit of his stomach. *What if Jory said no? Maybe he could invite the team? But what would they do?* There was no pool and no real garage. They'd have to be in the living room with Grandpa belching and farting. Or they could go downstairs to the drafty and mouldy-smelling basement. *Yeah, not a good plan.*

After getting out of the car, they slowly walked into the grocery store. Aiden hit the snack aisles, and ten minutes later he had what he wanted in the cart: protein bars, fruit, ice cream, tortilla chips and salsa. His mother was still going back and forth on so many things, and Grandpa was walking like a turtle down the aisles. Aiden pulled out his phone and saw he had a text from Jory.

can u talk?

sure

When his phone rang, Aiden said to his mother, "It's Jory. I'll be right back."

"Remember to invite him over."

Aiden nodded as he answered his phone. "Hey," he said, as he walked away from his mom and grandpa.

"I've got the best plan," said Jory.

"Oh yeah? What are you thinking?"

"I will vote for you if you vote for me. If there's two of us, maybe we can band together. Be a bigger team against Craig. If he gets named captain, which is what is going to happen, and we are alternates, we will at least have two votes against one. We'll need them, just in case he or his dad goes off again. His dad already tells him what to say and do all the time, but when he's captain it'll be way worse."

"Have you talked to anyone else?"

"No, but I think we're the most likely ones to get the 'A's. Don't you?"

Did Jory really think that? Aiden's heart sped up. He would do anything to be an alternate captain, he really would, but people here barely knew him. "Um, I'm not sure I am," he said.

"Oh, for sure you are. At least I think you are. And if we vote for each other, that might help. I bet I could convince a few others too."

"Okay." Aiden stared down at his sneakers and started shuffling his feet around. It felt wrong to be talking about this, trying to *make* something happen instead of letting it happen. Every other team he'd been on, the coaches had picked the captains and that was the end of it. And when he was little, the letters were rotated so that didn't count.

"We have a few seventh-grade kids on our team,"

said Aiden. "They might have a chance to be the leaders too, you know."

Jory started laughing. "I like how you say 'seventh grade' instead of 'grade seven.'"

"Yeah," said Aiden. "There are a few differences between Florida and here."

"I bet you never had a dad barge onto the ice before either."

"Never," said Aiden. *His dad sure hadn't been like that.*

"Okay, back to this captain deal," said Jory. "None of the older guys are that good, except for Tree. But he's the goalie, and goalies aren't usually captains. Let's just do this, okay? See what happens?"

"Okay. Hey, have you thought of any team names?"

Jory laughed. "Just the Misfits. That's what we are."

"Ouch."

"I know, I'm just kidding. What about the Degenerates? Or the Wacky Weirdos?"

"Come on, I bet you can think of something better than that."

"I don't see you coming up with anything."

"I know. We need something catchy though," said Aiden.

Aiden saw his mother coming toward him, her cart brimming with food and Grandpa walking beside her. Aiden's stomach rumbled. She motioned to

Aiden's phone and mouthed, "Did you invite him over?"

Aiden's mouth suddenly dried up. She wasn't going to let this go. *Come on, spit it out.*

"Did you want to come over one day?" His words came blasting out like paintballs.

"Sure, that'd be great." Jory answered right away, as if it was no big deal. "You can come over here one day too. Maybe I can go to your place after practice on Saturday, and then you can come to my place next weekend after we win our first game?"

"Sounds good to me," said Aiden.

When he pressed end, he thought that maybe the team drama would be okay if he at least had a friend to hang out with.

* * *

On Saturday morning, Aiden entered the kitchen and saw the big container of chocolate and vanilla cupcakes, iced and sprinkled and ready to go. Practice was at eleven, followed by the parents' meeting and pizza party. Then, after the party, Jory was coming over. Aiden was sweating already, thinking about what they would do in this drafty old house. *Would Jory think Aiden's house was weird and boring?*

Aiden got his bag ready and called out to his mom from the mudroom. "Time to go!"

Instead of his mother, Aiden's grandpa came in. "Have a good practice," he said.

"Thanks, Grandpa." Aiden furrowed his eyebrows and stared at his grandpa. "We're picking captains today," he said, just in case Grandpa wanted to talk.

"Just remember, a captain has to be a leader on and off the ice. Stick up for what you believe in, and be kind. That goes a long way."

Aiden's mother came around the corner, carrying the cupcakes. "It looks like a nice day out there," she said.

"If you like the cold," said Aiden.

"This isn't cold, honey. It's coming soon, though, so enjoy this while you can. Maybe you and Jory can play ball hockey outside this afternoon."

Was she as nervous as he was about having someone over? They hadn't really had any company since they'd moved in. A few people had brought over food in the beginning, but that was it. Mom said everyone was trying to give them space. When Aiden asked what she meant by that, his mother had said, "space to grieve." If space meant forgetting, then Aiden didn't want it, because he would never forget his dad.

He would also never forget how his dad died, or how badly he had handled it. Aiden shook his head. He didn't want to think about that. "Let's go," he said.

Outside, he opened the car door so his mom could

put the cupcakes in the back seat. Then he got in the front.

As they drove to the arena, Aiden scratched his jeans — over and over.

His mother glanced at him. "Would you like to be the captain? Even an alternate captain? I know this is a new team for you so that might be hard to accomplish, but it's okay to want it anyway."

Aiden stopped scratching. She must have picked up on his nervousness — or anxiety, as the doctors had called it. After his dad's death, he had to talk to a psychologist and *get coping strategies,* all because he'd had a meltdown — a panic attack, they'd said — and he couldn't sleep at night. He'd been okay lately and hadn't had a meltdown in a while. Unless a bad tryout counted. Did he want to be one of the captains? For some reason, he wanted it more this year than any other. *Why did he want it? To fit in? Be like his dad? Live up to the family name?*

"I guess I would," he said quietly. "But . . . I'll be U13 again next year, so I've still got another shot before I'm in the big leagues."

She smiled. "Oh, so U15 is the big leagues for you?"

"Well, yeah. That's when we start hitting. Well, at least the top teams do. I better make one next year. I hope I grow a bit before then."

"You will."

"You think I'll ever be as big as Dad was?" Aiden's dad had been six-foot-three.

"I don't know. We'll just have to wait and see. But however big you are, you'll be perfect to me."

Aiden rolled his eyes. "That is so corny, Mom."

She laughed, and he had to laugh too, because his mom sounded happier than she had in a long time. Was it because he was having someone over? Maybe their life was sort of getting a little better. It had been over five months now. Everything had happened so fast with his dad. Aiden shivered just thinking about the phone call. His mother screaming and crying, "No, no, no."

Aiden's mother had sold their house in Florida for way less than they bought it for. Aiden had heard the discussions between his mom and his dad's agent, and they were always about money — or Aiden. She talked a lot about how worried she was about him. He didn't want her to worry, but he knew she did when he was anxious.

* * *

There were a few guys in the dressing room when Aiden walked in. Manny was already half-dressed, and Aiden sat down beside him.

"I was here early," said Manny.

"That's great, man," said Aiden.

"And we do have a morning practice again next Thursday. Can your mother still pick me up?"

Aiden had forgotten to ask his mom, but he still said, "Oh, for sure."

While he was getting his equipment on, Aiden kept trying to steal glances at Craig. He was sitting beside Jory, and they were talking, but just with each other. *Had Jory asked Craig to do the same thing with the vote that he had asked Aiden to do?* If Craig voted for Jory, that would be two votes for him. *Was Jory just using Aiden?* Aiden bent over and pretended to tie his laces, even though they were already tied.

Whatever. He didn't care.

Only he did. His stomach started turning over and over, like a rolling wave. Water pooled behind his eyes. *Was his one friend already not his friend?* He shook his head and sat up straight. He had to think about practice and nothing else. Ever since his dad died, he had trouble controlling his emotions. He'd be okay, then bam, something would happen, and he'd be blubbering. *So what if Jory wasn't his friend?* He let his shoulders relax and tried to breathe deeply, just like the doctors had said, and it seemed to help. At least the tears didn't come out to embarrass him this time. Or worse.

Coach Ira came into the dressing room, and within seconds Coach Ben, Susie and Audrey were there too.

Coach Ira said, "I've got paper and pencils for everyone, and I want you to put two names on the paper, fold it up, and put it in the box. After practice, we will announce the captain and the alternates. And after the captains are announced, we will pick our team name."

"What if the guy the coaches pick for captain gets all the votes too?" Craig asked.

"We are asking for two names. So, we will take the votes, add them up, and make a list. It will all work out the way it is supposed to. Don't worry, we've figured this out."

Susie and Audrey were closest to the box, so they went first. The rest of the team lined up behind them, and one by one they wrote down their votes. When it was Aiden's turn, he wrote: *Jory. Susie.*

CHAPTER ELEVEN

AND THE CAPTAIN IS . . .

"I want everyone to start at a cone," said Coach Ira.

Aiden listened carefully because this was another drill he'd never done. At least without Mr. O'Brien on the ice, it was easier to concentrate.

"You are going to skate around the cones, with the puck," said Coach Ira. "Try to keep it on your inside. It's called puck protection."

"Usually we do this without pucks," mumbled Craig. "We need to skate." He sounded just like his dad.

When Coach Ira had finished talking, Aiden got up off one knee, picked up a puck, and skated to a cone. Soon, every player on the team was standing by a cone, and Coach Ira blew his whistle. Aiden skated around the first cone, then moved to the next, going around it in the other direction. It was harder than he thought, and he lost his puck. He picked it back up, then returned to the cone. Coach Ben had put the cones close together, and it took a huge amount of focus to weave in and out of them. It took a lot of edge control too.

Aiden heard skates behind him, so he picked up his

pace. As Aiden lost the puck again, Craig skated past him.

Aiden got back to the drill and chased Craig, trying to follow him and his foot pattern — his movement from front edge to back edge — but Aiden lost the puck a third time.

"Get up, J.J.!" Aiden heard Coach Ira yell. "That's it!"

"Manny-boy, chase it. Push through. Get back to your cones."

"Great edge control, O'Brien!"

"Keep going, Susie. You got this."

"Good job of getting back in, Aiden." Aiden pumped his legs, picked up the puck, and kept going. Finally, the whistle blew.

Sweat poured down Aiden's face as he sipped water over by the bench.

"That was hard," said Jory.

"Agreed," said Aiden. Even without Mr. O'Brien making them skate lines, Aiden's legs felt heavy and wobbly.

"Try doing that in goalie gear," said Tree.

"Sucks to be you," said Craig.

Coach Ira blew the whistle and called everyone over. "Okay, now we're upping the ante. Coach Ben is setting up an obstacle course, and I want you to watch him carefully as he goes through it. Once again you will be doing everything with the puck." Coach Ira put his hands to his mouth and yelled, "Go for it, Ben."

Aiden watched Coach Ben pass the puck under a board that was sitting on blocks, then jump over the board, pick up the puck, and go to the net. He wheeled around the back of the net, banked the puck off the boards, and raced to get it. Then he went around tires and jumped over ropes. To Aiden, the obstacle course looked super challenging.

"See when he goes over the ropes? When you're doing that, try to use your toes, like you're running on your skates," said Coach Ira.

"Running on skates? How stupid," said Craig.

"You guys ready?" Coach Ben called out.

"Whatever," mumbled Craig. "When I'm captain, I'm going to get them to stop with this garbage."

Aiden tried to ignore Craig.

"Find a spot," said Coach Ira.

Everyone got into position, and when the whistle blew, they all took off. Aiden put the puck under the board and jumped over it, but fell as he landed.

"Get right up, Mallory! Name of the game with this drill."

So, he did. Then he picked up the puck and raced toward the net. He wheeled around the corner and banked it off the boards, but he obviously didn't hit the right angle because it went straight out. Next time, he would get it right.

"No stopping!" Coach Ira kept up his banter to get everyone moving.

Players were falling all over the place, but Coach Ira got them up right away. The running was way harder than Aiden thought it would be, but Susie was great at it.

They went around once, then twice, then three times, then Aiden lost count. Finally, Coach Ira blew the whistle. Aiden bent over at the waist. How could a drill like this take as much energy as bag skating?

"That was a killer," said Susie.

"Quick water break," said Coach Ira. "Then put your sticks away because we're playing soccer."

"What?" Craig stared as Coach Ben threw soccer balls onto the ice.

"This is ridiculous!" someone yelled from the stands. "Make them skate. Make them work. Make them play HOCKEY!"

Aiden looked up. There was Mr. O'Brien with his arms crossed and a huge scowl on his face.

"Why did he have to show up?" Craig mumbled. Then he glanced at Aiden.

"Come on," said Aiden, "soccer will be fun."

The soccer game on skates was hard. The first time a ball came to Aiden, he kicked it and fell on his butt. He scrambled up and tried to go after it again. J.J. went up and down like a bouncing ball. Susie managed to pop the ball up in the air by using her knee instead of her foot. Then Manny tried to head the ball, but Craig came toward it at the exact same time and kicked both the ball and Manny.

Aiden held his breath. *Was Manny hurt?*

Coach Ira gave the whistle a screech.

Mr. O'Brien yelled, "What are you doing out there, Coach? This game is dangerous!"

Coach Ira looked totally frazzled. He skated over to Manny and helped him up. Manny nodded his head. Aiden exhaled. He was okay.

"Scrimmage time," Coach Ira said, with the soccer ball under his arm. Aiden could see the sweat on his face and the red blotches on his cheek. Soccer had been a bust.

As Coach Ira called out the lines, players hit their respective benches. This time Aiden was on a line with Susie and J.J., while Coach Ira put Craig and Jory with Manny. He kept the third line the same. Aiden figured he was going to be the second-line centre for the rest of the year, especially since the talk of Craig moving up seemed to have stopped.

"I can't believe we're with Doughboy," Craig said to Jory. Aiden heard the comment and knew Manny had too.

"Don't call him that," said Susie.

"Why? It's not like it's not true," said Craig.

Aiden glanced at Manny and saw his sunken shoulders. He skated over to him. "Remember how you got in front of the net at our first practice?"

Manny nodded. His face was scarlet, and his eyes looked watery. "I got a goal."

"Coach knows that. And yeah, you did get a goal by standing in front of the net. So just do that again. Go to the net and make sure you get between the goalie and the defenceman. Sometimes that can be hard if you have a good defenceman because they will want to push you away." Aiden's dad had been great at holding his ground in front of the net, screening the goalie. "If the defenceman won't let you get in between him and the goalie, stand in front and try to get your body in front of the goalie so she can't see. But don't go in the crease."

"Okay." Manny nodded. "I watched that on YouTube the other day. I know what the crease is. I've started watching hockey highlights now because I made this team. And games. My mom thinks I'm obsessed, and my brothers and sisters always want the iPad—"

"Good on you," said Aiden. He knew they didn't have a lot of time before they had to get skating again.

"Is it true your dad played in the NHL?" Manny asked.

Fortunately, Coach Ira blew his whistle, so Aiden didn't have to answer.

* * *

At the end of practice, Aiden followed Manny into the dressing room. "Nice goal," Aiden said.

"This time it went off my back." Manny laughed. His face was still red, but a different kind — red from working hard instead of from being embarrassed. Plus, he was excited. Aiden could hear it in his voice.

"We're going to start calling you garbage goals," said Jory. "G.G."

Manny laughed again, and this time Aiden joined in.

Aiden's line had scored three goals. Nice ones too. Aiden had even popped one in the side on his backhand, all thanks to Ned.

Once everyone had finished changing, Coach Ira and Coach Ben came into the dressing room with Susie and Audrey.

"Okay, listen up," said Coach Ira. "We're going to announce the captains now so everyone can go right to the party after changing. Before we do, I want to say that was a great practice. We have only one practice next week before we play our first game on Saturday." He did a couple of dance moves. "I'm pumped for our first game."

The team started cheering. Coach Ira laughed and put up his hands. "I totally agree with you that games are the most awesome part of hockey. We are going to kick butt! But we have to make every practice count too."

The cheering got even louder.

Coach Ben put his hands in his mouth and whistled so loud and shrill that everyone stopped making noise, and Manny even covered his ears.

"Nice whistle, Coach," said Tree. "Power plus."

Coach Ben bowed. "Thank you."

Coach Ira grinned. "Okay, now that Coach Ben got your attention, it's captain time. I'm going to start with our two alternates. We tallied the votes, and congratulations . . . drum roll please." Coach Ben started the drum roll, and soon the entire team was on board.

"Jory! You are our home alternate captain."

Everyone cheered and laughed as Jory stood up and did a funny bow like he was tipping his hat and tap dancing.

"Hey, that's better than my bow," said Coach Ben.

"Um, Coach, you barely even did a bow," said Jory. Then he broke out into a dance move. Coach Ira allowed the room to keep laughing before he put his hands up again.

Suddenly Aiden's heart was beating frantically under his T-shirt and his palms were sweating like crazy. *How could he go from laughing his head off to sweating like it was a thousand degrees in the room?* He hated when this happened. *Breathe.*

Why was he panicking? He'd told himself he didn't care.

His heart thumped and he was sure everyone in the room could hear it. He inhaled and looked at his knee, which was jiggling up and down. *Breathe.* He exhaled.

"Drum roll please . . ." The drum roll started again, and Aiden joined in, but this time he wanted it to keep going forever. *What if his name wasn't called? What would everyone at the tournament think?*

"Our away alternate captain is . . . Susie! Congrats, Susie."

Aiden's heart fell to the end of his toes. That was it. He wasn't an alternate captain. He exhaled.

There was cheering but not like it was for Jory. As disappointed as Aiden was, he was happy for Susie, so he cheered along with the rest of the team. She didn't bow, but she did her dance that got her long braid swinging like a horse's tail.

"And now for our captain," said Coach Ira. "This should be the biggest drum roll, please and thank you!"

Coach Ben started the drum roll, and Aiden slapped his legs just like everyone else so no one would see how crushed he was. The sound was so loud it bounced off the walls. Did everyone feel the way he did about how disastrous Craig being captain would be?

"The captain of our team . . . who was chosen by me and Coach Ben . . . because of his work ethic and dressing-room skills . . . more drum roll . . . is . . .

CHAPTER TWELVE

SPEECHLESS

"Aiden Mallory!"

Aiden froze. Had he heard right? He couldn't have heard right. *No way. Not a chance.*

He . . . he had to be imagining things. *It had to be Craig. He was the best player on the team.* He'd lapped Aiden today, breezed by him. He was the only one who could kick the soccer ball without falling.

What had just happened?

Aiden didn't say a word, nor did he move a muscle — not even to look around the room. The other players were cheering. Loudly. He could hear them, but it was like he was outside the room listening in.

Suddenly, it hit him—

He was captain!

"Come on, Mallory," Jory said, nudging him with his shoulder. "Get up and do a dance or something."

As much as Aiden hated being in front of a crowd, he knew he had to. He was *captain*!

He stood up and was about to do an awkward dance move when Craig yelled, "This is so RIDICULOUS! He only got picked because he's a suck-up and his father was in the NHL! And because of the stupid tournament! Like his father even deserves to have a tournament named after him."

The room hushed. As if he was on autopilot, Aiden sat down. He stared at the floor.

"O'Brien, can it," said Coach Ira. "That's not the reason, dude. We've been watching, observing all of you, and Mallory works hard on the ice, never complains. He comes to the arena early, is always the first one to take the ice, and he talks to other players in the dressing room and on the ice, encouraging them to be better. That's what we want in a leader."

The team cheered, but Aiden's throat had dried up completely, so he took a swig out of his water bottle instead. *Could he handle this?* Handle Craig and Mr. O'Brien breathing on him, telling him every mistake he made?

Once the noise had been brought down by the coaches, Aiden knew he had to speak.

"Um, thanks," was all he said. *He'd never be a good captain saying something stupid like that.*

"I, um, won't let you down," he added.

"We know you won't," said Coach Ira.

"Bow time." Jory tossed tape at Aiden. "You don't get off that easy. Show your moves, Mr. C.!"

"Yeah, Mr. C., we need a dance," said Manny. "I'll

show you how." He jumped up, but he still had one skate on, so he almost toppled over.

Aiden sucked in air. He really, really hated doing stuff like this, but he stood up. He'd do a dance if he had to. He had just been named captain, after all!

But before Aiden could bust out in a move, Craig stood up, hauled his bag over his shoulder, and headed for the door. He stopped right in front of Coach Ira. "This is WRONG, and you know it. You probably just want a signed jersey from a dead guy. I bet Flor-i-dian offered you that as a deal. A signed jersey from a guy who died in a car accident from DRINKING AND DRIVING!"

He stormed out of the dressing room, swinging the door so hard it banged against the concrete wall.

Silence filled the room and Aiden found his seat. His eyes burned. *Why was this happening again? It wasn't true. It just wasn't true.* His dad had stopped at a pub for lunch on his way to a charity event, but he didn't have a drink. People had taken photos with him, and when someone on social media posted a photo they'd taken with him under the pub sign, it had exploded. The comments started coming in about how he'd been drunk when he had his accident. Drunk! *None of it was true.* They'd proved he hadn't been drinking, but it didn't matter because social media had blown it up. In some ways Aiden was still mad at his dad for even stopping at a pub and posing for a photo. His dad always, always stopped if he was asked. *Why didn't he say no just this once? Why didn't he go through McDonald's for lunch instead?*

More than that, why had he died? He'd left Aiden and his mom to pick up the pieces. Didn't he know how hard it would be?

Aiden didn't want to see the look on anyone's face — the pity or the judgment. He'd seen that already, back in Florida. After his dad died, no one knew how to talk to him. And tons of people made horrible comments like Craig just did. People who didn't even know his dad said things without caring about the truth. Social media had been flooded with lies.

Even his friends had believed what people were saying. They'd make dumb jokes that weren't funny to get rid of the silence. Now it was happening again in a different city, a different country.

The awkward quiet of the room was broken by Coach Ira saying, "That was uncalled for, and not true. I'll deal with O'Brien once he cools off. Okay, the rest of you, get dressed and we'll see you upstairs for pizza and cupcakes. Congratulations, Aiden. You're going to make a great captain."

"What about picking our team name?" Manny asked.

"We can do that another day," said Coach Ira.

The dressing-room door was open and shut in

seconds. Were the coaches going to find Craig and make him apologize to Aiden? Well, he didn't want an apology. He just wanted to . . . what? What did he want? Go back to Florida without Dad there? They couldn't do that because of Grandpa. They had to move here. Plus, there were too many memories in Florida, as his mother had said.

For Aiden, there were too many memories everywhere.

Maybe what Aiden needed was to quit hockey. *Just forget about it. He could never live up to his dad. Ever.* Especially being back here, where he was constantly reminded about how great his dad was.

And that he had died.

And how he had died.

Aiden picked up his skates and placed them in his bag.

Once the coaches had left, the drone in the room started again, but it was slow, like a beehive just waking up. *Had he been picked because of his dad? What if he couldn't do this? What if he couldn't make the team perform? Work in practice? What if he wasn't any good? He would be such a disappointment.*

Aiden didn't want to talk about a team name, and he didn't want to hear what anyone was saying. He was captain and he knew he should talk, but his throat felt like it was closing in, his airway narrowing. No words could squeak out if he tried. He sucked in a deep breath and shuffled the equipment in his bag. He couldn't look up or around, look anyone in the eye. And he *tried* to ignore what they were saying, but he could hear them talking about him, about his dad, in little whispers. Tears pooled behind his eyes and Aiden knew he had to get out of the dressing room. *Now.*

Suddenly it was as if he couldn't get enough air. Like the air going to his lungs was trying to sneak through a straw. He was taking short, quick breaths, trying to get anything to his lungs. This was how he'd reacted after his father had died. *He couldn't have a meltdown. An attack. Not now. Not here. He just couldn't.* He had to get out of the room, but it was swallowing him whole.

He quickly zipped up his bag. J.J., who was sitting beside him, whispered, "I voted for you. You're the one who should be captain."

Aiden nodded but didn't speak.

Jory sat down on Aiden's other side. "Don't listen to O'Brien. You can do it. I voted for you too. But I didn't need to because the coaches picked you for captain. Captain! That's amazing. Congrats!"

Jory's words seemed to float in the air. Aiden couldn't even smile at him because he could barely breathe.

The air in his throat now felt as if it was moving

through a pinhole. *Was he going to faint? Right here in the dressing room? What if they called an ambulance and he ended up in the hospital? That would be so embarrassing. Was he going to hyperventilate? Was he going to just collapse on the floor in front of all his teammates?* Aiden stood and picked up his bag, then he ran out without saying a word.

He stumbled down the hall and ducked into the deserted Zamboni area. He dropped his bag and gasped for breath. He knew he *was* hyperventilating. Stars started to swim in front of his face. *This had happened before, and he'd got through it. He could get through it now too.* He leaned his head against the cool wall and put his hand to his heart, trying to slow it down. It was racing out of control. He balled his hands into fists until his nails dug into his palms. But he wasn't supposed to do that. He had to relax his shoulders. He tried. He let his hands fall to his side. He tried to breathe. In and out. *Come on, air.* In and out. *Breathe.* His chest heaved. His airway opened a little, but still not enough to breathe normally. He inhaled and exhaled. *He could do this.*

He squeezed his eyes shut but tears sprung out anyway. Down his cheeks, like waterfalls. His shoulders started shaking, and the sobs began. He hated this. He really did.

Everything circled around his brain. *His dad. The cops coming to the house. The funerals. The awful comments. Drinking and driving.* Obviously, people here believed that too.

Forget about that part. He had to. He had to. He had to.

The tears kept flowing and his shoulders shook.

Here was his big chance to do something, to be a captain, and he'd already blown it. *Maybe it was better his dad wasn't here to see what a loser he was.* He hadn't said a word of leadership to his team. Nothing. Nada. Zilch. *No. He had to stop thinking about bad things. He should have stood up and had everyone talk about a team name. Made it fun.* His throat started closing again. His heart ached. *How could he make something fun when he felt like he was covered in something so heavy it was hard to breathe?*

Come on, air. In and out. In and out. *Breathe.*

Then he felt the hand on his shoulder.

"Are you okay?" Ned's gentle touch and the tone of his voice made Aiden calm down a little. He kept breathing in and out. He unclenched his hands and tried again to do the relaxing-his-shoulders thing.

Just the presence of Ned made Aiden feel as if his windpipe was opening up, wider and wider. He was okay. He was getting enough air. He was. *Was it over?* He wiped his face with his sleeve. "I'm . . . fine," he finally said.

"I know when someone is having a hard time," said Ned.

Aiden nodded. He put his hockey bag over his shoulder. "I have to go home," he said. Except home was a drafty old house in the middle of nowhere. Aiden wished he and his mom had moved to a place where no one knew anything about them.

"I thought your team was having a pizza . . . party. I helped clean up the room."

"I don't want to go."

"That's a bad attitude."

"I don't care."

"Then why are you crying? If you didn't care, you wouldn't have to cry."

"I wasn't crying." Aiden discreetly tried to wipe his cheeks, to get rid of the telltale signs.

"I saw you got a backhand goal in . . . scrimmage today." Ned held up his hand.

None of this was Ned's fault, so Aiden high-fived him. "Yeah, the practice helped."

"That's good."

The happiest Aiden had been in Prairie Field was that morning with Ned — just the two of them and a fresh sheet of ice. "Can we practise again?" Aiden said. "Just thirty minutes?"

"You weren't upset like this when we practised," said Ned.

Aiden nodded. "That's why I want to go again."

"If it will make you smile, maybe we can even go out two times," Ned said. "When the pond freezes, we'll play outside, but for now we'll go . . . inside to get you ready for that first game." He smiled at Aiden.

Aiden liked talking about his dad with Ned. So as much as he worried it was wrong to go on the ice early, he still wanted to. He wiped his face again. Just talking to Ned had helped his heart rate and breathing go back to normal.

Ned tilted his head and stared at Aiden. He had such a confused look on his face that his wrinkles were like deep grooves. "I don't like seeing you like this," said Ned.

"I wish I could talk to my dad," said Aiden softly.

"You can." Ned put his hand on his heart. "Because he's here. He's with me. I can feel him. So, he has to be with you too."

Aiden nodded and exhaled. "Yeah." He lifted his chin and stared at Ned. "The coaches made me captain today."

"That's . . . *fan-taaaas-tic!*" Ned patted Aiden's back. "You'll be good. I watched your daddy and know what he did. He always helped his teammates, even the guys who weren't as good. Sometimes he'd go on the outdoor ice and . . . practise with guys to make them better. You can do that when it gets cold. I'll help."

"I'm not the best player on the team," said Aiden.

Ned tapped his chest. "You've got what it takes here. That's most important." Then he clapped his hands. "This is the best news of the day. You wear that 'C' with pride. It's an . . . honour!"

Aiden was about to reply when he heard a voice. "Hey, Mallory, there you are!" Coach Ira said, as he came around the corner. "I've been looking all over for you."

"Ned and I were just talking." Aiden couldn't look Coach Ira in the eye. *Was his face a blotchy mess?*

"Yup, we're having a good old chit-chat." Ned patted Aiden's back again. "He'll be as good a captain as his daddy was."

"Or even better," said Coach Ira. "I picked him because of what I saw, not because of his dad. This decision was all about leadership." He put his arm around Aiden. "Come on, Mallory. We've got pizza and cupcakes to eat."

"Sure," said Aiden. He tried to wipe his face again before he turned to Ned. "Thanks," he said.

Ned cupped his hands around his mouth and whispered in Aiden's ear, "Monday. Six."

Aiden glanced at Coach Ira, but he wasn't paying attention to what Ned was telling Aiden. "Thanks, Ned," Aiden said again.

"I have to apologize for something," said Coach Ira, as he and Aiden walked down the hall. "I made an announcement about a tournament not knowing you weren't in the room."

"You mean my dad's tournament?"

"Yeah. You know it's named after your father?"

Aiden nodded. "Prairie Field is kind of a small town. It's okay," he said. "When is it, anyway?"

"In a month. There's going to be a silent auction, and they've got some amazing stuff rolling in for it. Could make a lot of money for the arena. Your mom donated a few of your dad's jerseys to auction off, and local businesses are keen to help out too."

Aiden nodded. It was a month away? *What if he couldn't improve in time?*

"I also had a talk with O'Brien," said Coach Ira.

"Don't make him apologize," said Aiden.

"Yeah. Okay, agreed. But he needs some consequences. What he said wasn't cool."

"It's not true, you know."

"I know, dude. I read all the reports."

Aiden glanced at Coach Ira out of the corner of his eye. "Please don't make a big deal of this," said Aiden. "With O'Brien, that is. Just let it go."

Coach Ira put his hand on Aiden's shoulder. "Not something you need to worry about."

"But . . . I'm the captain."

"Yeah, but that doesn't mean you have to be involved with this kind of thing. You deal with the dressing room and having some fun on the ice."

"Did you think it would be like this when you decided to coach us? There seems to be a lot of *drama*, as my mom would say."

Coach Ira laughed. "Not even close. I thought I'd get a bunch of kids in grade six and seven, and we'd just be laughing and joking while winning hockey games."

As they got close to the stairs, Aiden saw the hockey bags all grouped together. He dropped his by the others, then hesitated.

"Do the parents know anything about what happened?" he asked. If Aiden's mother knew, she might go storming over to Craig's house and give his father a piece of her mind.

"No. I would like to keep what was said in the room between us, as a team. We will deal with it as a team. And I will deal with it."

"I'm with you on that," said Aiden. "My mom is a bit protective since my dad . . ." His words trailed off.

"Yeah, I get that. By the way, your mom makes killer cupcakes." Coach Ira slung an arm around Aiden. "Now, come on. Stop worrying. Pizza!"

CHAPTER THIRTEEN

CUPCAKES AND SUPERHEROES

The smell of gooey cheese and pizza dough hit Aiden as he walked up the stairs to the party room. As soon as he entered, his mom immediately stopped talking and headed his way.

"Hi," mumbled Aiden. "Did you, uh, go to the parents' meeting?"

"I did, and so did Grandpa," she said.

"Grandpa's here?" Aiden looked around the room, then saw his grandpa sitting at one of the old wooden tables with brown metal legs — the kind you had to fold up and stack. It looked like it had been around since Grandpa played hockey at this arena. The room had plaques on the walls, and Aiden figured they probably hadn't been dusted in years.

Lots of people surrounded his grandpa. Aiden kept forgetting he was a hero in Prairie Field too.

Just like his dad.

There it was again: his dad occupying his thoughts.

"It was a good meeting," she said. "I like your coaches. They wanted Grandpa to come because they were announcing the tournament. The Luke Mallory Memorial."

Aiden nodded. *Did she know he wasn't in the room for the announcement? Maybe she hadn't missed him. Did his face show that he'd been crying? She couldn't find out he'd had a panic attack or she'd hover over him.* He tried to make conversation. "You, um, you don't think they're too young? Like everyone else does. My coaches?"

"Not at all. They're keen. They'll be fun. And they seem to be organized. Obviously Mr. Ramos and the minor hockey association think so too or they wouldn't let them coach." She lifted Aiden's chin. "Is something the matter? Have you been crying?"

Aiden jerked away. "Mom, don't," he hissed through clenched teeth.

"I'm sorry," she said. "But most of the players were here with their parents. Where were you? I wanted you to come up with me for the announcement."

So she *had* noticed he wasn't there. "With Ned." Aiden spoke sharply. "He wanted to tell me something about our practice. I didn't miss it on purpose."

"Okay. You don't have to talk to me like that." She paused. "Your teammates were so excited when they heard about it. They really cheered."

Aiden's shoulders sagged. Now he kind of wished

he had been around. "They could have waited," he said. *Why did everything good have to be bad?*

"Honey, they couldn't. Some parents had to leave. And the pizzas had arrived. The coaches didn't know you weren't in the room."

"I'm sorry," said Aiden.

She put her hand on his shoulder. "I think I'm right that something is up."

"Let it go, okay? I'll fill you in at home." He would fill her in, just not on his panic attack.

"So, introduce me to Jory," said his mother, in a forced cheerful voice. "I should meet him before he comes over."

Oh no. Aiden had totally forgotten he had invited Jory over. "I'm not sure he's still coming," he said.

He glanced around the room. Where was Jory? Aiden couldn't see him anywhere. He also couldn't see Craig. *Had the two of them left together?* Aiden yanked out his phone. He had no messages from Jory, but a few from his Florida friends. He would text them later and tell them he was captain. They were so far away that they didn't have to know he'd already blown it.

"Did something happen with Jory?" his mom asked slowly.

Aiden shook his head at her. "Stop. I'm hungry," he

said, shoving his phone back in his pocket. "Is there any food left?"

"I'm sure there is." She put her hand on his shoulder. "Honey, I'm excited for the year and all the fun things being planned. This tournament is a nice gesture for your dad and leaves a good legacy. It could end up being a big deal in the future."

"I know," said Aiden.

Since she hadn't mentioned him being captain, she obviously hadn't heard yet. He would tell her at home. He *should* tell her now, but Aiden didn't want her doing her big congratulations with a hug and kiss. Plus, she already thought something was wrong, so she'd be confused and start asking more questions. *And there was the fact that he'd already bombed.*

Aiden saw Susie over by the boxes of pizza. "I'm, um, going to get some pizza," he told his mom.

"Sure," she said. "Go be with your friends."

Friends. *Probably not anymore.*

Aiden headed over to the table, and when he got there, he said, "Hey."

What else was he supposed to say? *Sorry for walking out? For being a bad captain? For crying like a big baby? For being so sensitive about his dad? For almost having a panic attack? For actually having a panic attack?*

"Hey," Susie said back. "That is so neato-cool that

the tournament is named after your dad! I can't wait."

Leave it to Susie to move on like nothing had happened. *How long had he spent talking to Ned? It sounded like so much had gone on without him.* Susie tilted her head and looked Aiden in the eyes. He wanted to duck his head, to turn away, but there was no way she was going to let him do that.

"Neato-cool?" He made a funny face at her. "Did you really just say that?"

"Yup, I did." She paused, but only for a second. "So . . . that was awful what Craig said. I think he might *actually* feel bad. But who knows — it's Craig. Anyway, I know you'll be a good captain. Jory and I are going to be with you all the way."

"You talked to Jory?"

"Sure did. We're a team." She held up her fist. "Captains work together."

He had to bump it back. "Where is Jory?" Aiden asked, scanning the room again. His grandpa was surrounded by even more people now.

Susie craned her neck to look around the room. "I don't know. He was here. Maybe he's in the bathroom? Boys always have to poop. My brother sits on our toilet for hours."

"Um, too much information. Did, um, O'Brien go home?"

"Let's just say that his dad wasn't too happy about *anything*, so they both went home. Coach Ira said it's okay. He'll phone and get things straightened out. But he did talk to Craig about what he said to you. Or at least I think he did. He must have. He's the coach. I would have if I was the coach."

"Yeah, I bet you would have."

She put her hands on her hips. "And what is *that* supposed to mean?"

"Nothing." Aiden picked up a paper plate and a piece of pizza.

"Ohmygod!" Susie squealed. "I almost forgot to tell you. Your mother's cupcakes are the best! I could have eaten them all, every single one. I liked the chocolate best though."

Aiden laughed out loud, and it felt okay. "She lets me have only one when she's making them, so I can't wait to have another one."

"You're kidding, right? There's none left. They were gone as soon as she put them down. Whoosh."

"Seriously?"

"Would I joke about something like cupcakes?" She laughed. "But, hey, there's pizza left. I'm starving."

As Aiden was loading his plate with a second slice of pepperoni pizza, Jory jostled him with his shoulder. "Your mom makes the best cupcakes!"

"That's what I said," said Susie. "I want ham and pineapple." She moved down the pizza table, lifting the lids on the boxes until she found the one she was after.

"Am I still coming over to your house?" Jory asked Aiden.

"Um, sure, but you don't have to if you don't want to."

"Why wouldn't I want to? Just 'cause you didn't take a bow, you big chicken? I'm going to teach you a dance, and you will do it next time. But yeah, I already talked to my parents, and your mom talked to mine. They'll pick me up later."

Aiden nodded. His stomach was getting woozy again. *What if Jory thought his house was boring?* His palms started sweating.

"My parents love your grandpa," said Jory. "They've been talking to him since they got here."

"I hope he's making sense," said Aiden.

"He's telling some good old hockey stories," Jory said. "Hey, so cool about the tournament." He bumped Aiden. "It's named after your dad!"

Fortunately, Aiden didn't have to reply because Susie returned with a plate loaded with pizza.

"Hungry much?" said Jory.

"I worked hard today. More than I can say for you. You didn't kick the soccer ball once."

Jory playfully bodychecked her. "I didn't want to get hurt."

"Heeeeeey, don't. I can't drop my pizza!"

Aiden pointed to a table next to his grandpa's. J.J., Manny and Tree were already sitting at it. "Let's get a seat," he said.

As they walked over, Jory said, "We should have a captains' meeting to plan a team party. I can have it at my house."

"And Aiden's mother can make cupcakes," said Susie.

They sat down on the folding chairs, with Aiden ending up beside Manny.

"Your mom—"

Aiden interrupted Manny, laughing a little. "She makes the best cupcakes, right? Was that what you were going to say?"

"How did you know?" Manny asked.

"I can read minds," said Aiden.

"Me too," said J.J., as he squeezed his eyes shut, put his hands up, and waved them like he was a fortune teller at a fair. "And I can see into the future that we are going to win our first game of the season and the game after and the game after that and the game after that."

Aiden laughed so hard he almost choked on his pizza. When he had recovered, he said, "You got that right." He paused, then blurted out, "We need a team name first!"

"Yeah, we do," said Tree.

"I'll talk to Coach Ira, and we'll figure it out next practice," said Aiden. "So, start thinking. We need something that sounds awesome when we cheer before the game."

"Yeah, something super cool, like we're superheroes or something," said Manny.

"Superheroes?" Tree laughed and threw a balled-up napkin at Manny. Manny laughed too as he ducked. The napkin went flying behind him just as Coach Ira walked by.

"Hey, no throwing garbage." He picked it up and tossed it back to Tree. "Garbage, dude. What's this about superheroes?"

"We still need to vote on a name for our team," Aiden said.

Manny held up his hands. "We're a superhero group!"

"Superheroes are cool!" said Coach Ira.

"There are so many." Manny bopped in his chair. "We could be one of the obscure ones."

"Obscure?" Tree asked. "How do you know all the obscure ones?"

"I read a lot of comic books," said Manny. "I'm not talking Batman or Superman. What about Lightray or Human Torch or . . . or . . . Martian Manhunter?"

"Martian Manhunter!" Jory slapped his leg. "Can you imagine us all sticking our hands in the middle and saying, 'Let's go, Martian Manhunters, Let's go'? The period would be over before we got through our cheer."

Coach Ira laughed along with everyone, Manny included, for a few seconds. Then he said, "Keep thinking, team. We do need a name. We were going to do that today but . . ."

Everyone looked uncomfortable. The reminder of what had happened in the dressing room hit Aiden square in the gut. In that moment he wished he had the superpower to be invisible. But no go. It all flooded back: The comment from Craig and then the silence. Aiden walking out, panicking, crying on Ned's shoulder.

The table had suddenly taken on an awful, agonizing awkwardness because he had a dad who died. He had to say something. *This was his chance to redeem himself.*

"But we didn't," said Aiden, with as much cheerfulness as he could muster. *Did his words come out higher than normal?* He had to continue. "Can't do everything in one day. It's like homework."

His joke worked, and Coach Ira laughed. "I'm with you on that one. Which reminds me, I've got to get going. Grade twelve is a killer. I'll be up all night. See everyone on Thursday. Just one more practice before puck drop!"

When he was out of earshot, Jory said, "I've never had a coach who is as excited as me for the first game."

"Me either," said Aiden.

"I hope O.B.'s dad backs off a little when the games start," said Tree. "I'm glad my dad's not like that."

Aiden wanted to say, "I'm glad my dad isn't either," but he couldn't get it out because the words were actually "I'm glad my dad *wasn't* either."

So instead he said, "O'Brien's on our team. We have to make this work."

CHAPTER FOURTEEN

FIRST VISITOR

"This is my bedroom," said Aiden. *This was so awkward.* Jory had come over, and Aiden was showing him the house — not that he thought there was much to show.

"Whoa! You have so much hockey stuff," exclaimed Jory. "This is so awesome. Like, awesome of major proportions!"

Awesome? To Aiden this was normal. All his old friends had hockey stuff on the walls of their rooms, so Aiden's wasn't a big deal. He had jerseys from the five NHL teams his dad had played on, framed and hanging on his walls. And there were a few signed photos of his dad's old teammates. When they'd moved in, Aiden's mom had put up some shelves for Aiden's own trophies and photos too.

"You have a signed Crosby photo!" Jory darted over to the wall and stared with his mouth open. "This is mind-blowing!"

"My dad only played with him for six months," said Aiden.

"Still! Wait until I tell the team."

Tell the team? "Hey, um, maybe we should just keep this to ourselves."

Jory turned to Aiden. "Dude, why? Your dad was a legend. There's going to be a tournament named after him!"

"I don't know." Aiden shoved his hands in his pockets. "I don't want them thinking I'm . . . I'm different, I guess. Or to remind them I should be better at hockey than I am."

"Okaaaay, I'll keep it quiet, but I'd tell everyone if it was me."

Jory went over to Aiden's shelf and picked up a photo of his team from last year. "What was it like playing in Florida?"

"Different," said Aiden. "We went to the arena in shorts all the time."

"I mean playing-wise."

"Not as many kids played. Basketball and baseball are way bigger. Football too."

"Did you play any other sports?"

"Just baseball for a couple of years. Since my dad was off all summer, we travelled and stuff, so my parents didn't like the commitment. If you sign up, you have to play all summer long. Baseball is intense down there, like hockey is here. My dad liked to boat too, so we did a lot of that." Aiden wasn't sure why he was rambling. *Why was he so nervous?*

Jory put the photo back on the shelf and picked up another one, this time of Aiden's hockey friends at his house, playing in the pool.

"Is this your pool?"

"Yeah."

"You were rich!"

"Lots of people have pools there. It's kind of normal," Aiden said. "Um, let's go downstairs."

"And do what?" asked Jory.

"I dunno. We can go outside and shoot balls. I have nets by the side of the house."

"Okay."

As they were heading downstairs, Jory's phone pinged. He pulled it out of his pocket and gave it a glance before putting it back. "O.B. That's, like, the fifth text."

"Is he okay?"

"Yeah. He's just being a dink."

"Why?"

"He's so full of himself but then he's not really. He acts tough, but my parents think he's not as tough as he tries to be. He knows I'm here, so he has to text, like, a trillion times."

"Have you played on teams with him a lot?"

"When we were five, we played on the same team. That's when we first became friends. Then in first-year U11, we made the same team again. I had such a good tryout that I made the two team, and so did he. Then the next year he made the one team and I made the two team. *Again*. Who does *that*? Only me, of course. Loser much?"

"That's something I'd do." Aiden paused for a moment. Then he asked, "What's he like? O'Brien? Like, really."

"He's O.B. Always been like he is. But he has two sides. My mom thinks I should be nice to him. She feels sorry for him because his dad is so hard on him. When he's at my place, he's chill, totally different. So he can be okay sometimes."

The television was blaring when they got to the bottom of the stairs. "Sorry. My grandpa likes the television loud," Aiden said.

Jory started laughing. "So do my little brother and sister."

"How many brothers and sisters do you have?"

Jory held up two fingers. "Twins. A boy and a girl. They're a pain most of the time, except Christmas morning. Then they're fun. They just turned six a few weeks ago. Their birthday party was painful — there were a million screaming kids."

"I wish I had a brother or sister. Would have made this move easier."

"I've never moved. We've always lived in the same house."

"I've moved so many times."

"Sometimes I think it would be fun to move somewhere like Florida. It would be cool to live in a different city."

"It's not all that fun, believe me," said Aiden. "Mom," he called out. "We're going outside to play ball hockey."

Aiden's mother came out from the kitchen. "Sounds good. You boys play outside, and when you come in, I'll have a snack ready."

"Cupcakes?" Jory asked. "Mrs. Mallory, you make the best cupcakes."

Aiden's mom winked. "I was thinking something else. Something better than cupcakes."

"Sundae bar!" said Aiden.

"Go outside." She laughed.

Out on the driveway, Aiden and Jory set up one net. Then Aiden had an idea, something that was like what he did with Ned. "Why don't we put targets on the net and try to shoot at them? We could play a game for points and see who wins."

"Great idea. We could see how many we can hit and get points for making each target. What could we make them out of?"

"Cardboard?"

"Okay. How will we secure them on the net?"

Aiden thought about this. "String? I think it will

work." He ran into the house and came out with a cardboard box, some string and a pair of scissors. Once they had the targets done, they tied them onto the net.

"These might not last more than one shot," said Jory.

"Whatever. Let's give it a try."

Jory shot first and misfired. The plastic ball went sailing behind the net. He ran over and stickhandled back with it. Aiden got ready for his turn. When he shot, he grazed the very bottom of the target.

"Hit!" Aiden called.

"I *guess* that counts as a point," said Jory. "But let's do five points if you get a bull's eye, and different points for different areas."

They kept playing, shooting at the targets and each missing lots but getting some. Aiden hadn't had this much fun in a long time. He was about to take a shot at the top corner when a car slowly drove by his house. In the front passenger window of the car, he was sure he saw Craig's face — and he didn't look happy.

"Uh-oh," said Aiden.

"What? You doing that **uh-oh-ing** 'cause you're going to lose, big time? I'm still up by one, and you'll never catch me." Jory laughed and did a dance.

"No. I think Craig just drove by."

"Seriously?" Jory squinted at the car as it kept driving down the street. "Yup, that's his dad's car, all right." Just as Jory spoke, his phone pinged. He yanked it out of his pocket. After looking at it for a moment, he shoved it back in. "Yup, he's mad."

"Oh no. That's not good."

Jory shrugged. "Whatever. I'm up by a point. Let's just keep playing."

* * *

Jory's mom came to pick him up at five o'clock, but then stayed and talked with Aiden's mom for at least twenty minutes. When Jory was finally leaving, he said to Aiden, "Thanks for having me over."

"You'll have to come to our house one day," Jory's mother added.

"I'd like that," said Aiden.

Jory tapped his forehead with his palm. "Oh, I forgot to tell you, Mom. I'm having a captains' party at the house one of these days. We have to figure out a time."

"Sure," she said.

Once they were gone, Aiden put the net away and went back into the house. His grandpa was at the kitchen table waiting for dinner, so the television was finally off. Aiden's mom had already set the table, and a big salad sat in the middle. She was standing over by the oven, wearing her oven mitts.

Aiden sat down in his seat next to Grandpa, who was at the head of the table. Aiden's mother brought over a platter of chicken and roasted potatoes. She set it on the table, then dished some onto Grandpa's plate.

"Dad, did Aiden tell you he's going to be the captain of his hockey team?"

She eyed Aiden as she spoke, and he knew that look. Busted. He stabbed a piece of chicken.

"And when were you going to share that good news with me?" she asked Aiden, her eyebrows arched way up on her forehead.

"Sorry," he mumbled. "I forgot."

"Forgot about something that important?"

"Something came up," said Aiden.

"What would that something be?" She stared at him, and he couldn't look away.

"Can't say. Sometimes what happens in the dressing room stays in the dressing room."

"Oh my god, you sound just like your father."

Aiden's grandpa put his hand on top of Aiden's and winked at him. "That's my boy. You're going to make a good captain."

"Thanks, Grandpa." Aiden hoped this was true, but then he thought about Craig.

What would he be like at school on Monday? Craig had had a double whammy. Both the "C" for his jersey and Jory had ended up with Aiden today.

CHAPTER FIFTEEN

BALL HOCKEY

Aiden got on the bus on Monday morning after an early practice with Ned. It was getting easier to wake up for hockey, but not easier to wake up for school after going back to bed.

He saw Jory right away, but not Craig. *Good thing.* Aiden made his way to the back.

"Hey," said Jory, sounding half-awake.

Aiden sat down beside him. "Hey," he replied. "Where's O.B.?"

Jory rolled his eyes. "His dad bought ice time in a town fifty clicks from here. They go on the ice and practise by themselves."

"For real?"

"No lie," said Jory. "He did it last year too. He makes him go on the ice and skate drills. Sometimes he makes him skate with his laces untied. Craig said it's something about being good for balance or edge control or something. Sounds kind of weird to me, but his dad knows an NHL skating coach, and he told him it was good. They invited me last year, but my parents said no. *Of course.* They're the fun police. My mom was like 'not during school hours.' Man, I would have gone for sure. Anything to get out of school."

"How often do they go out?" Aiden was a bit shocked. Buying ice time for just one person?

Jory shrugged. "Last year it was only a few times. But this year O.B. said it would maybe be twice a week because his dad is so mad that O.B. made such a low team. He said he needs more practice. Plus, we get such lousy ice time. Only one this week."

"My mom told me our team was voting on buying extra ice time," said Aiden. "Coach Ira is trying to get some out of town. Well, the parents are voting since they're the ones with the money."

"Yeah, my parents told me that too. They aren't sure how to vote." Jory rolled his eyes. "They say they already pay enough, so I'll just have to convince them. I can't believe O'Brien's dad buys ice just for him. Wish my parents weren't so strict about school."

"My mom too." Aiden would do anything to miss school for hockey. And it might beat getting up at five thirty, although he was sure no one could help him like Ned had.

Craig still hadn't arrived when the noon bell went, so Aiden rushed to catch up with Jory as he walked out of the classroom. Maybe today he could hang out with him at lunch.

"Hey, you want to sign out the sticks and play ball hockey?" Jory asked.

"Sure," said Aiden.

They went to the equipment room and picked up two sticks, signing their names on a sheet of paper that was being monitored by an eighth grader. Then they headed outside.

Teams were already being formed, and Aiden stood back a bit, waiting for someone to pick him. His stomach started to flip. *Why did he always hang back?* He had to change that. He was captain of a team now. During their ice time that morning, Ned had told him a few things his dad had done when he was captain in Prairie Field.

"You," said an older boy, pointing at Aiden. "My team."

Aiden nodded. His throat went dry. He had been split up from Jory.

The game had just started when Aiden saw Craig running across the playground with a stick in his hand.

Craig glared at Aiden before he said, "I'll go *against* Flor-i-dian."

A seventh grader on the other team gave Craig a nod. "Sure, O.B., you're with us."

Since there were no refs, the ball was just dropped

and batted at, and whoever won the battle took off with it. Aiden ran up and down the pavement, barely touching the ball.

Finally after a few minutes, he saw it rolling his way. He sprinted toward the ball, picked it up on the end of his stick, and ran with it, looking for an open teammate. He saw a kid racing forward and shot him off a pass. The kid rifled the ball and sunk it into the back of the net. Aiden put his hands in the air. "Great goal," he called out.

"Yo, nice pass, dude," said the boy.

On the next play, Aiden got the ball again. This time Craig ran up beside him and tried to knock the ball off Aiden's stick, but Aiden put it between Craig's legs.

He was about to dart around him and run up the side when he felt a hard push against his back. Not expecting the hit, Aiden lost his balance. He slid forward, crashing to the pavement and skidding on his knees. Sharp stones stuck to his kneecaps and the palms of his hands. Although his knees were stinging and his sweatpants were ripped, he scrambled up and turned around.

"What?" Craig smirked. "I barely touched you."

"What was that for?" Aiden's knees burned like they were on fire. Blood trickled down his shins. He shook his hands to get the little stones out of them.

"We're just playing a game," said Craig. "If you can't handle it, go play *superheroes* with your baby friends."

Had Jory said something to Craig about Manny wanting to name the team after superheroes?

"Get back in the game or get out," said an older kid. Then he glanced at Aiden's knees. "Nice shred. Get those cuts cleaned."

"Yeah, yeah," said Aiden. "When the bell goes." He glared at Craig. "Let's play."

Aiden sucked it up and ran up and down, passing the ball as best he could and staying out of Craig's way. But was he ever relieved when the bell rang. By then he had blood all the way down his legs and in his socks.

When he got back into the school, Aiden went to Mr. Rowland and asked if he could go get cleaned up.

"Go ahead, but how'd that happen?" Mr. Rowland asked.

"I fell."

"Okay. Away you go. Tell them to put some antibiotic cream on those cuts."

* * *

"Aiden, can we have a word after class?" Mr. Rowland had stopped by Aiden's desk with only ten minutes until school let out.

Aiden nodded while his stomach did a backflip. *Teachers don't just say they want to see someone to have a chit-chat about nothing.*

"What do you think he wants?" Susie whispered,

after Mr. Rowland had gone back to his desk.

Aiden shrugged. "No idea. But I kinda rushed through my outline." Mr. Rowland had returned Aiden's essay outline with a lot of red slashes and a mark of ten out of twenty. There was no way his mother could find out. In Florida, Aiden had always got As.

"I bet that's it. Fingers crossed," she whispered. "Jory told me Craig pushed you playing ball hockey."

"No, I fell," said Aiden.

Aiden could barely concentrate and kept looking at the clock. Nine more minutes. He wrote a few things down. Five more. As the minutes ticked by, Aiden's stomach got sicker and sicker. *Did Mr. Rowland want to talk about what had happened at lunch?* One more minute and school would be over. Aiden wanted to get home, go over to the arena, and hit balls against the wall — not stay after and talk to the teacher.

The bell rang. Aiden pretended to be busy picking out his homework books, but while everyone else was leaving, he was staying.

"Teammates don't rat," whispered Craig as he walked past Aiden's desk.

Aiden ignored Craig and kept his head down. His leg jiggled, and he could feel the sweat dripping down his back, his heart rate starting to rev. *Breathe.* There was no way he could let this turn into another meltdown.

As the rest of the kids filed out chatting about school and hockey, Aiden drew squiggles on a piece of paper.

When the class was empty, Mr. Rowland said, "You can come up to my desk. I don't bite."

Aiden gathered his books and walked to the front of the room. Seeing a teacher after school was new to him. His stomach felt like bugs were crawling around in it, trying to get out.

"You didn't put a lot of effort into your outline for your personal essay," said Mr. Rowland. He sat forward in his chair, his hands clasped.

"I know," said Aiden.

"Any excuses? I'm used to excuses."

"Not really." Aiden shrugged. "I was tired."

"That's pretty standard for a hockey player." Mr. Rowland paused, and Aiden didn't pick up the slack. He just stood there, wanting the conversation to end.

"I'm going to go out on a limb here." Mr. Rowland's voice sounded softer now, a little more forgiving. "I have a feeling this is a difficult assignment for you."

Aiden refused to look at Mr. Rowland and instead stared down at some random paper on his desk. He couldn't read anything on it. The words were all blurry.

"I'm okay with your topic," continued Mr. Rowland, "even though it's about hockey. But how about you try to add a little more to it and expand on why the move was so hard from a personal perspective. In other words, whether you wear shorts or jeans to practice isn't something you'll be able to write an entire paragraph about. That's the weather. Maybe add something about what's it like to fit into a new school or a new hockey team. The personal part behind that. Do you understand me?"

Aiden nodded.

"Now, I'll let you hand in your outline again, okay? I understand you're new to our school, and you've been through a lot in the past few months. You can hand it in to me tomorrow and I'll re-mark it."

"Thanks," said Aiden.

Aiden rushed out of the classroom and made it onto the bus just in time. Jory waved to him. He was sitting beside Craig. Aiden made his way to the back and sat in the seat behind them, pretending as if nothing had happened.

Immediately, Craig turned around, gave Aiden a nasty smirk, and asked, "Hey, Flor-i-dian, what'd Roly want?"

"My outline sucked."

Craig slowly nodded as if he didn't believe Aiden. "I got nineteen out of twenty on mine," he said.

"What are you writing about?" Jory asked him.

Craig shrugged. "Not making the team you're supposed to make."

"Oh," said Jory. "I thought we weren't supposed to write about hockey?"

"I can, because it's personal."

Aiden glanced at Craig and saw his smirk was gone.

"I got seventeen because I'm writing about annoying twins," said Jory. "Like how they get into my stuff all the time. Yesterday they wrecked my entire room. I flipped on them and then my mother flipped on me. So not fair."

"They are annoying," said Craig. "But kind of cute too. Do they miss me? I haven't been to your house in ages."

"Maybe. They did ask about you the other day," said Jory.

"Then invite me over." Craig playfully punched Jory on the arm. "I'll play with them."

Aiden stared at Craig. *Play with little kids?* Craig must have sensed Aiden eyeing him because he turned and looked at him again.

"What are you writing about?" Craig asked Aiden.

"Moving," he replied.

CHAPTER SIXTEEN

FOOTPRINTS IN THE SNOW

Snow was falling when Aiden snuck out of the house early Wednesday morning. The ground was covered in a layer of white that made the streets look clean and fresh, like just-washed bedsheets. He could still feel the softness and warmth of his own bed as the cold penetrated his jacket, making him shiver.

He'd just have to run fast, he decided, to build up some body heat.

As Aiden ran, his footprints made a pattern in the snow behind him. He had to admit, the snow looked sort of magical as it sparkled through the darkness. According to last night's weather channel forecast, it was supposed to continue until around ten, then the sun was coming out. Aiden's mom kept saying the real snow was coming soon.

As usual, Ned was waiting for Aiden at the front door of the arena. He ushered him in quickly, then locked the door behind them.

"I'll go get ready," said Ned.

"Me too," said Aiden.

Half of the lights surged on as Aiden tied his skates. He snapped his helmet on, put on his gloves, and stepped onto the ice. Even though it was a horrible time to get out of bed, Aiden liked the quiet and stillness of the empty arena. To him it was peaceful. He didn't have to think about anything else, like school or Craig or his dad. He could just skate.

Ned clunked onto the ice in his full goalie gear, and their shooting practice began. They did the same drills over and over. Ned said practising the same thing was good, that it built muscle memory. Sometimes Aiden couldn't believe how smart Ned was and how much hockey sense he had. Ned knew hockey better than anyone Aiden knew, except maybe his grandpa.

Aiden was aiming for the top corner when Ned stood up straight and put up his blocker. "Don't shoot. Did you hear that?"

"Hear what?" Aiden asked.

"The door. It sounds like someone is banging on it."

Aiden stopped stickhandling to listen, and sure enough he heard it too. Then he heard someone trying to push the door open. His heart started to race.

"We . . . have to get off the . . . ice," said Ned. His speech was really slowing down. Aiden knew that wasn't a good thing. "I . . . have to turn off the . . . lights. We . . . have . . . to go!"

Ned skated so fast to get to the boards that Aiden trailed behind him.

"The net," whispered Ned. "Get the . . . net off."

As quietly as he could, Aiden put the net back where it belonged while Ned turned off the lights.

Aiden sat in the dark arena, his body shaking and heart racing, and tried to untie his laces. *Breathe. Breathe. He couldn't freak out. Not now.* His fingers were having a hard time working. *Who was at the door? Were they in trouble? What would happen if they were?*

Since he had moved to this town, all Aiden was doing was getting into trouble. First school, now this.

Once Aiden had his skates off, he didn't know what to do. *Should he leave?* He didn't want to run into whoever was at the door. Ned, now out of his goalie equipment, came over to the bench where Aiden was sitting.

"I think they're gone," said Ned. "I heard a . . . car."

"You sure?" Aiden asked. His heart was just starting to return to normal. His breathing was slowing down. He'd managed.

Ned nodded as if he was thinking. "You need to go out the . . . front door. Same door you came in. Let's sneak over and see if anyone is there. Go . . . behind me. It's okay if I'm in here but maybe not you."

Aiden followed Ned to the doors and stood in the shadows as Ned peered out, his face pressed against the glass. "No one," he said. "No cars and it's dark." He turned to Aiden. "It's nothing. Now . . . scoot home."

Aiden just nodded. "Um, thanks, Ned." His voice squeaked. "For the target practice."

Ned opened the door, and Aiden slipped outside. He took a quick look around, and sure enough he saw footprints — bigger ones than his. And just his luck, Aiden's old tracks hadn't been covered by snow yet. *Had it been Mr. Ramos?* No. The president of the minor hockey association had keys. He wouldn't have to bang on the door.

Aiden took off running. By the time he got to his house, he was panting like he did after the hardest shift of his life. His chest pounded and he bent over at the waist to catch his breath.

Aiden tiptoed up the back stairs and creaked open the door. Then he slid inside and slipped out of his soaking-wet sneakers and socks. He padded through the kitchen and over to the stairs.

He was about to go up the first step when he heard a voice. "What are you doing up?"

Aiden's stomach flew to his throat. He whipped around to see his grandpa standing in the dark.

"Just getting a drink of water, Grandpa," said Aiden.

"Oh, okay."

"What are *you* doing up?"

"Heard a car," he said. "And needed a drink."

"I'm going back to bed now," said Aiden.

"You do that." Grandpa turned and headed to his favourite recliner in the living room.

At the top of the stairs, Aiden's mother came out of her room, tightening the belt on her robe and brushing her tangled hair off her face. "What's going on? It's six thirty-five."

"Nothing," said Aiden. "Grandpa and I were just getting water at the same time."

"Okay. I'll go down and make sure Dad is okay, and you go back to bed for an hour."

Aiden flopped on his bed and stared at the ceiling. His heart pounded through his skin. *Keep breathing. Slow and steady. In and out.* Through sheer will he slowed his heart down. Then he tried to sleep but instead just stared at his ceiling, thinking about what had happened.

Could they get in trouble?

* * *

Fortunately, Aiden's grandpa had a morning appointment, so Aiden's mom dropped him off at school on their way. He yawned as he walked in and Manny came running over to him.

"Is your mom still going to pick me up tomorrow?" Manny asked.

"Yeah, no problem," said Aiden. He'd still forgotten to ask her, but she said she would help.

"I should probably give you my address." Manny rolled his eyes a little. "And my mom wants to call your mom so they can arrange it."

"Sure, okay," said Aiden. "I'll make sure my mom calls tonight. Or your mom can call her. Whatever works."

Manny bobbed up and down on his toes. "What time do you think you'll come?"

"Like five forty-five? Practice is at six thirty. How far are you from the arena?"

"Ten minutes if my dad drives, but fifteen if it's my mom."

"My parents were the opposite," said Aiden.

"That's funny," said Manny.

Yeah, and my dad was the one who died in a car crash.

Manny stopped laughing and shifted his gaze to Aiden's right shoulder. "I gotta get in the classroom," he said.

Aiden pivoted to see who had made Manny so nervous. He frowned when he saw Craig.

"I'll walk in with you," Aiden said to Manny.

"You will?"

"Sure," said Aiden. They started walking and were almost at the classroom door when Craig caught up to them. "How's it going, *team*?" he asked. He slung his arm around Aiden.

"I'm good," squeaked out Manny. "I won't miss practice tomorrow. Aiden's mom is picking me up."

Aiden was about to say something to Craig when Susie barrelled into the conversation. "Did Mr. Rowland want to talk about your outline?" she asked Aiden, breathless.

"Yeah, he did," said Aiden. "I fixed it last night."

"I got twenty out of twenty on mine," said Manny.

"Good on you," said Aiden.

"What did you write about that was so interesting?" Craig asked Manny.

Uh-oh. Aiden wondered how Manny would get out of this one. He was writing about bullying, and Aiden didn't have to be a genius to know who he was talking about.

"I'm so pumped for our game on Saturday," Aiden interrupted, before Manny had the chance to answer.

"Don't get too excited," said Craig. "We only have one practice this week. So brutal. Hopefully he can get some ice time out of town."

"My mom says we have to pay extra for that," said Manny.

"So?" Craig jabbed Manny in the upper arm. "You tell her to buck up. We need the practice."

Manny put his hand to his arm. "Okay, okay."

"One more practice tomorrow morning," said Susie, "and then it's time! I'm beyond pumped. I've never been on a team that had this many practices before the first game."

"And some of us are putting in even more practice." Craig nudged Aiden with his shoulder again. "Right?"

"You're lucky," said Aiden. "My mom would never let me miss school to practise."

"That's not what I meant," said Craig.

CHAPTER SEVENTEEN

DRESSING–ROOM DYNAMICS

"Where does this boy live?" It was still pitch black out, and Aiden's mom was driving down a long gravel laneway, their car bouncing through potholes.

"Obviously in the boonies," said Aiden. He had been slouching, trying to grab another five minutes of sleep, until they had hit the dirt road. Now he was wide awake.

"Okay, we're coming up to something," said his mother.

"There's Manny," said Aiden.

"Oh my goodness, he's standing in the dark. Not even an outdoor light is on." She leaned over the steering wheel and peered out the window. "This is quite the old farmhouse."

Even in the dark, it looked like it was falling apart. In the beams of the headlights, Aiden could see stuff all over the yard. Bikes and toys and strollers and boards and even a car. Nothing looked like it worked. Manny waved at them as Aiden's mother stopped the car so he could get in. She popped the trunk, and Aiden pressed the window down.

"Hey, Manny. Throw your stuff in the back," he said.

"Thanks for picking me up," Manny said, when he got in the car.

"No problem," said Aiden's mom. She drove forward a little, trying to find a decent spot to turn around. Aiden hoped she wouldn't run over anything in the dark.

"My mom can't drive me because my dad's not home and she can't leave my brothers and sisters," said Manny.

"I'm happy to keep picking you up," said Aiden's mother. "Am I okay to turn around here?"

"I don't want to miss any more practices," said Manny, as if he hadn't heard her. "I've never been on a good team before. And we have that big tournament coming up. I'm so pumped for it. It's named after your dad. That is so cool. I looked him up yesterday — he was really good!"

"We'll make sure you get to practices," said Aiden's mom. She cranked the wheel and got the car heading in the right direction.

A few cars were already in the arena parking lot when they pulled in. It had taken longer than Aiden thought to pick up Manny.

"We better hustle," Aiden said, as he got his bag out of the trunk. Then he quickly yanked Manny's out too. He handed it to him along with his stick.

"Thanks," said Manny.

"No problem, but let's hurry," said Aiden.

As it was, when they got to the dressing room, the rest of the team was already getting dressed.

"Hey, Flor-i-dian, nice of you to show up," said Craig. "Last I heard the *captain* of a team should be the first one in the dressing room. Already slacking, I guess."

"He had to pick me up," said Manny.

"No one asked you, Doughboy."

"Can it, B.O.," said Tree.

Craig spun around. "What'd you call me?"

"Oh, right, it's O.B.," said Tree. He grinned and flexed. Craig scowled at him but sat down.

Aiden dressed in record time so he could be the first one on the ice. He stood and made his way to the dressing-room door. Craig followed so closely behind him that Aiden could feel Craig's breath on his neck.

Aiden turned. "Let's have a good practice," he said, addressing the room. It was his first real comment as captain.

"How profound," said Craig.

Aiden ignored him and headed out onto the clean ice. All of the lights shone brightly this morning, unlike when he practised with Ned. The sound of his skates on the ice made Aiden relax and breathe and feel free.

As soon as he rounded the first corner, though, he heard the arguing. Mr. O'Brien was standing at the end of the ice with a man Aiden recognized as Mr. Ramos. What was the president of the minor hockey association doing at an early morning practice?

"You can't go on the ice. We have selected our coaches," said Mr. Ramos. "They will run the practices and the team."

Had he got up early just to come and stop Mr. O'Brien from putting on his skates and ruining another practice?

"Uh-oh," said Jory, skating up to Aiden. "Here we go again."

As they skated away from the fighting and got back on the straightaway, Aiden said, "Let's not let it bug us."

"Easy for us, harder for Craig," said Jory.

Aiden searched the ice for Craig, wondering if he was hanging his head again. But no — he was at the far end of the arena, surrounded by Mason, Colin and Bilal. Aiden wondered if Craig had even seen — or heard — his dad yet. Craig leaned in and said something to Colin. Aiden saw him laughing and then the others started laughing too.

The whistle blew. Now Craig's dad was shouting, and Coach Ira had to talk over the off-ice battle. Players kept glancing over, so Coach Ira clapped his hands.

"Eyes on me!"

When Coach Ira had everyone's attention, he said, "Listen up. This is our last practice before we play on

Saturday. We need full concentration and full effort from every player. Today we are going to skate and do technical work for the first half. Then we will work on cycling the puck and a breakout drill to get ready for the game."

"Are we going to do power play?" Craig asked.

"Not today. That'll come later once we have a few games under our belt."

"You have no clue," muttered Craig. Aiden heard some of the guys snicker. *What was happening? Were there splits in the dressing room already?* Aiden had heard his dad talk about splits in a room, and how much they could hurt a team.

The first drill was skating and passing with partners. Coach Ira blew his whistle. They skated and skated, up and down the ice, passing the puck back and forth. Coach Ira was a stickler for keeping their feet moving, even with the puck on the stick. After passing, they moved on to other drills, until finally there was a water break. Aiden sucked back a huge gulp and wiped his mouth, then he snapped his cage back in place.

Now it was time to cycle the puck. Aiden was with Susie and Bilal today because Coach Ira had moved Manny back to defence and put J.J. with Craig and Jory. As much as Aiden wanted to be on that top line, he wouldn't say anything. He knew how important it was to respect Coach Ira's decisions.

They got into position, and Coach Ira said, "Keep the puck moving. Get it on your stick and make the pass. Fast, fast. I want it moving around and around. If you miss the pass, skate hard to pick it up and get it on the stick of your linemate. Now go!"

"We can do this," Aiden said to his group. He was positioned behind the net, with Susie along the boards, Bilal at the hash marks, and Manny and Colin on the blueline. Aiden passed to Susie. She sent the puck back to Manny, who passed it to Bilal. He skated around the net with it and gave it back to Aiden. Then Aiden gave it to Colin and they went the other way. They made the puck go around and around.

"Crisp and clean," yelled Coach Ira. He blew his whistle. "Forwards, change your positions. Ds stay on the blueline, but we'll swap Mason in for Colin. Colin, it's your turn to shoot pucks against the boards and practise backwards skating."

Aiden moved to the wall. Every time he sent the puck back to Manny, he got it on his stick and shovelled it off. Had Coach Ira seen that Manny could be a decent defenceman? He was like a brick back there.

"Just like your daddy, dishing it back like you're having a tea party." Without Aiden noticing, Mr. O'Brien had moved and was now standing on the other side of the glass, right behind him.

Aiden sucked in a deep breath and tried to shut out the voice, but it was hard.

Coach Ira skated over and said, "This is not your practice."

"Sure, kid. What do you know? I played this game. I know. He's a lightweight just like his old man was. And to think they named a tournament after him. Now that's a joke."

Coach Ira shook his head. "You shouldn't have to deal with this," he said to Aiden.

"It's okay," said Aiden. "I'm not listening." Only he had heard everything.

Then Coach Ira muttered under his breath, "Why can't they just kick this guy out?"

After the scrimmage at the end of practice, Aiden picked up the pucks. He knew this was part of being a captain. This he could do, but the thought of talking to the team again made him feel sick.

Going into the dressing room, Aiden's throat went dry. He had to talk to his team, but he didn't really know how. *It wasn't like he was funny or smart.* His brain buzzed with what he could say, what he should say. *Why didn't he prepare something ahead of time?*

When everyone was in the room, he knew he had to say something. So he said, "Great practice. Great, um, effort out there."

"What a pathetic thing to say," said Craig. "You sound like a robot."

"R2-D2," said Bilal. Then he made a robotic noise.

Aiden ducked his head. *He was terrible at this.*

"We don't have a team name yet," said Manny. Aiden silently thanked Manny for changing the subject.

"Let's think of one now," said Craig. "How about the *Superheroes*? We could all wear capes!" Aiden knew his mocking tone was directed at Manny. Colin, Bilal and Mason started laughing.

"We shouldn't pick now," said Aiden. "Susie and Audrey aren't here."

"So? They're *girls*," said Craig. He stood up. "Who thinks we should vote now?" He looked at Mason, who put up his hand. So did Colin. Then Bilal slowly did too.

Aiden's heart started to race. *How was he going to deal with this?* Craig was taking over the room, and not in the right way. Aiden had no experience being a captain. He knew he had to say something. Anything. *Why did the coaches pick him?*

Aiden cleared his throat. "Susie and Audrey are part of our team. And Susie is our alternate captain, voted in by the team."

"Oh, right, I forgot about that," said Craig. "I sure didn't vote for her."

"Can it, buddy," said Jory. "Mallory is right."

"Oh, so now you're calling him Mallory?" Craig sat back down, shaking his head like he was totally disgusted. "You think you can get close to the NHL because of him?"

"Whatever," said Jory. "I'm playing U13 hockey. On team three, in case you've forgotten. I don't have big dreams to make the pros, I just want to play. Anything wrong with that?" Jory threw a wad of tape in the trash can. "By the way, you're on team three same as me, so good luck with those NHL dreams."

Then Craig threw a wad of tape right at Jory, hitting him in the cheek. "You're so two-faced," he said. "Anyway, I know a secret about your little hero Mallory."

"Shut up, O'Brien!"

"You shut up!"

Aiden knew he had to do something. Anything. There was going to be a fight in the dressing room, and Aiden had to stop it.

Aiden stood, his legs shaking. "Enough," he said, hoping he sounded stronger than he felt. "It doesn't matter what team we're on. We're still a team."

Craig started snickering. So did Mason, then Colin and Bilal joined in.

"What a dweeb," said Craig. "Did you get those lines from a *captain's manual* or something? One of your grandpa's books from a thousand years ago?"

The dressing-room door opened. Aiden breathed a sigh of relief when Coach Ira and Coach Ben walked in. He sat down, his hands shaking and his heart freaking out. He'd never done anything like that before. Not that he'd done it well. He should tell the coaches he wasn't cut out to wear a "C."

"What's going on?" Coach Ira furrowed his eyebrows and glanced around the room.

"Not a thing," said Craig.

"We need to pick a name," said Aiden, his voice quivering. "But we need Susie and Audrey in here first."

"We do need a name!" Coach Ira said. "Let me go get them. They're dressed already."

"Coach, my dad is waiting. I have to get to school. Need those grades!" Craig said in a sickly sweet voice.

"Point taken," said Coach Ira. "Let's meet fifteen minutes early on Saturday and pick a name before the game. I'll send an email to your parents."

Aiden undressed quickly. They still had to take Manny home, so he wouldn't have much time to get ready for school or eat breakfast. After slinging his bag over his shoulder, Aiden said, "See you guys on Saturday for a win!"

"Wow, such leadership, *Captain*." Craig rolled his eyes.

Aiden walked out with Manny, his head down. They

had only gone about halfway down the hall when they ran into Ned.

"Hey, Ned," said Aiden.

"Top of the morning to you!"

"Ned," said Aiden. "Do you know Manny?"

"Yup. He's played here for a few . . . seasons now."

"You know me? That's so awesome." Manny grinned.

"Hiiiii, Ned." Craig had caught up to Aiden and Manny. Bilal and Colin followed him like they were his groupies. "Watch out for those *banana peels*." They all laughed and kept walking.

When Aiden looked at Ned, he had his lips clamped together and was shaking his head. Aiden put his hand on Ned's arm. "It's okay, Ned. He was just joking."

"I work hard to keep this arena . . . clean. It's . . . it's not a joke to me!"

CHAPTER EIGHTEEN

WEIRD CONVERSATION

"What's the matter?" asked Aiden's mom, after they had dropped off Manny.

Aiden ran his finger along the car window.

"Aiden? Did you hear me?"

"Yeah. I heard you."

"Is there something wrong?"

"No!"

"Hey," she said. "That doesn't sound like nothing's wrong."

Aiden sighed. "I'm not captain material."

"Sure you are." The car bumped through another pothole. At least the sun was coming up, so Aiden's mom was swerving to miss a few.

His dad had been swerving too.

Aiden slouched and crossed his arms. "You're my mom — you have to say that."

"What's going on? Talk to me, okay?"

"I don't want to tell you because I need to deal with it by myself." Aiden sighed again. *Or with Dad, but he's not here anymore.* "It's complicated. I just don't think I'm good. That's all. I'm not like Dad. I get nervous when I have to say anything, and then I say the wrong things."

"You don't have to be like Dad. Just be yourself."

"Do you know how hard that is? Craig should be captain. He has a bunch of the guys following him like they're gum stuck on his shoes. It's so hard, and I just don't know the guys all that well."

"Your coaches saw something in you. Don't give up."

"Well they're stupid if they saw something in me. I'm lousy."

"Don't say that."

"It's true." Aiden slouched lower in his seat.

They drove the rest of the way in silence. Then as they turned down their street, Aiden got up the courage to ask something he'd wanted to for long time.

"Mom?" said Aiden softly. "This might be a weird question but . . . do you ever talk to Dad?"

She pulled into the driveway and shut off the car but didn't move to get out. Instead she turned and looked at Aiden, putting her hand on his shoulder. "I go to his grave almost every day just to talk."

"You do?" She'd never told him. She never took him. But then . . . now that he thought about it . . . she had kind of mentioned it once, and he'd run to his room. At that time, it had just sounded creepy . . . and too hard to do. That was way back in the summer though. The psychologist told him he didn't have to go until he was ready.

"Yeah, I do," she said. "I still need him. He helps me. Gives me advice on Grandpa and you. And me too."

"Isn't that kind of weird? Won't people think we're the loony family?"

She gently touched his cheek. "No. Not at all."

"Do you think I could go?" he asked. "I need to talk to him."

"Sure. When would you like to do that?"

"I dunno. After school?"

"I'll pick you up."

Aiden gave her a little smile. "Can you drive me to school too? Like, now?"

She smiled back and gave him a playful punch on the shoulder. "Give a little, take a lot. Yes, I can and I will."

* * *

After school, Aiden waited at the front doors for his mom to come and get him. When Jory had asked if he was catching the bus, Aiden said he had to go somewhere with his mother. Aiden had wondered if Jory was going to invite him over on the weekend — until he heard him and Craig talking about going swimming. So much for their captains' party and Aiden getting invited somewhere. *Why was being captain so hard for him?*

Aiden's mom pulled up, and he got in the car.

"How was school?" she asked. This was always her first question.

"I got seventeen out of twenty on the outline for an essay I'm doing for English." He didn't dare tell her his first mark. Didn't matter now. All that mattered was this mark.

"What's the essay on?"

"It's supposed to be personal, so I'm writing about moving from Florida to here and what the differences are. Like how hockey is different, and how I feel playing hockey here versus there."

"How *do* you feel?"

"I dunno." He stared out the window, not wanting to talk anymore.

"Did you still want to go to the cemetery?"

Aiden nodded. Fortunately, his mother must have picked up on his mood — or she was in the same mood — because they didn't talk the rest of the way there.

Aiden's father had had two funerals. The first one was in Florida and a ton of people came, including all kinds of players from the Panthers and from the other NHL teams he'd been on. There had been almost a thousand people there, and it was in a big auditorium with flowers and a stage. Tons of people had given speeches, like coaches and even his trainer. All the photos on the table up front were of Aiden's dad in his NHL jerseys, and there was a slide show with so many pictures of Aiden and his mom, on the boat and at games. One was Aiden as a baby in a Montreal jersey. Afterwards there was a catered lunch with so much food, even things like prawns and fancy dips. Aiden ate one chicken finger and then barfed it up. For him the entire event had been like a big blur. So many people to shake hands with and tell him they were sorry, people he didn't even know. Then near the end, he'd had a meltdown. He'd lost it big time. Some people had called it a panic attack because he could hardly breathe, gasped for air and his heart had raced out of control. Then when it did slow down and his throat had opened, he'd had some weird yelling fit, and he threw things. After that he'd gone to the doctor, and then a psychologist. He'd fought going, even though it ended up helping.

The second funeral was in Prairie Field, and it was smaller and at the arena. Lots of people came from Prairie Field and from other small towns and cities, and there were lots of men his dad had played junior hockey with. It was different though. People brought homemade food and placed it on the old wooden tables with checked tablecloths. The local church had donated white plates. They had big photos of his dad from when he played junior hockey, but also from when he played bantam. There was even a photo of Aiden's dad with Ned. And one of him and Grandpa, of course.

Then they had buried his ashes in the Prairie Field cemetery. This time Aiden hadn't had a big meltdown, but he'd cried until his shoulders shook. His mother had fretted, thinking he was having another panic attack.

The funerals seemed so long ago, and so did saying goodbye. Now here Aiden was, going to see his dad's grave and, what . . . say hello again?

The Prairie Field cemetery was located on the edge of town. It was behind the church, but far back, and filled with all kinds of headstones — new ones like his dad's, and old ones too. Some were even babies from ages ago. Aiden had read some of them to get away from thinking about his dad when they had come to bury his urn.

They were pulling into the cemetery parking lot when Aiden said, "I think it's harder here. Harder to make teams."

His mother quickly took her gaze off the road and glanced at him. "I didn't expect you to answer."

"I'll let you read my essay after I've written it."

"I'd like that." She cruised into a parking spot and shut off the car.

They sat in the car for a few seconds in silence. Then his mother said, "I brought some flowers."

"Okay."

"Do you want me to go with you? Or did you want to go by yourself?"

"Come with me," Aiden said.

They got out of the car, and Aiden carried the flowers. They walked side by side, almost in stride, without talking, as they went toward his dad's headstone. When they got to it, they stopped.

"You can put the flowers beside his name," his mother whispered.

Aiden walked toward the grave and laid them down, blinking back tears. He didn't know it would be so hard to see his dad's name engraved in the big stone. He exhaled and went back to stand by his mom's side. His mother took his hand in hers and gave it a little squeeze. He squeezed back and glanced over at her, and that's when he saw the tears running down her face. A pain stabbed his heart.

"I'm going to make the flowers pretty for him," she said.

"I'll help."

They knelt, and Aiden's mom snipped the bottoms of some of the flowers and put them in a little vase that was sitting beside the grave. She gave Aiden a few of the roses and told him to place them how he wanted. So, he did. One here. One there.

"That looks nice," she said, when he was done.

"Thanks," he whispered.

"Did you want to talk to Dad by yourself?"

"I think so," said Aiden.

"Okay," she said. She stood up and wiped the dirt off her jeans. "I'll go get some water for the vase."

Aiden lowered his head. "Thanks," he said again.

She patted his head as she walked by. After she'd left, Aiden knelt there for a few minutes, not really knowing what to say. Finally he blurted out, "I'm so mad at you. But I miss you so much."

He waited. And waited. And waited. Tears fell down his face.

"Did you hear me, Dad? I miss you. I'm not doing very well at anything. School or hockey. I hate that you died. Why did people say mean things? Why did you have to . . . swerve? That's what I'm . . . mad about. And that you just . . . left me . . . and Mom."

Aiden waited. Why was he doing this? Babbling to the air.

I miss you too, Bud. And I'm sorry. It was instinct to swerve.

Aiden sat up straighter. Could he really hear him or was he imagining things? He wanted it to be real. "I need you so much right now," he whispered.

I know. I'm so sorry.

"I was made captain of my hockey team." Aiden played with one of the flowers that he had set out. He swished it back and forth like a broom. He didn't want to talk about that horrible time anymore. He needed to talk about now.

You'll be great.

"I don't think so. I don't know how to be good. I'm not a very good talker in the dressing room. I hate that stuff. I need you here to tell me what to do."

Lead by example, not words.

"But . . . I'm not the best player."

Doesn't matter. You can lead by example in other ways. Remember, always try your hardest and don't give up. And treat every teammate the same, with respect and kindness. Kindness goes a long way.

"There's one guy, Dad, and he's mean. Horrible to some of the other guys. But it's not his fault — or I don't think it's all his fault. Well, it is his fault, but he does it because someone is mean to him."

Even those ones, Bud. But don't let that kind of player walk all over you either. That's the balance. Stand up for what you believe in.

"Okay."

You can do it. I believe in you.

Aiden inhaled, the fresh air hitting his lungs. "My team is in a tournament named after you. What if I play lousy and embarrass you? Embarrass your name?"

You could never embarrass me. And don't think like

that. *Play your game, not mine. You're a much more skilled player than I ever was."*

"I don't think so. I made the three team."

I made a team like that one year, when I was around your age. The year before I moved to Prairie Field to live with my uncle. My dad was being hard on me, and I just couldn't perform in the tryouts because I knew what awaited me at home. I held my stick way too tight. You've been through a lot, Bud. Give yourself a break and just work on getting better this year. This year will be a learning curve for you. Next year you will fly.

Aiden had never thought too much about his dad having obstacles when he was young because Aiden had only ever known his dad as a pro player. And he'd been a star in juniors and in Prairie Field. Aiden knew his father had moved because of the abuse at home, and maybe Aiden had heard this story before but never really listened because what difference did it make? His dad had gone on and made the NHL. But now . . . it did make a difference.

"I'm sorry your dad was mean to you. I get it now, after seeing a dad be awful."

I've forgiven my dad now.

A lump formed in Aiden's throat. "I forgive you too," he whispered. "For dying. And for leaving me." Tears rolled down his face.

Aiden closed his eyes for a second as he exhaled. Then he craned his neck to look at the blue sky. It was like something had been lifted off his shoulders. He felt okay now. He wiped his face.

Did the crocodile live?

What? Aiden looked at the grave, at his dad's name. "Did you really just ask me that?"

I did. Why not?

"Because it's a ridiculous thing to ask."

Aiden's father had been driving to a charity event when he had swerved and hit a tree, all because he was trying not to hit a crocodile that was crossing the road. People made a joke of it and said he must have been hammered, drugged up, drunk out of his mind to swerve for a reptile. He should've run it over, they'd said. Those comments hurt. Aiden's dad had died trying to save something. Social media had been so mean. So many people had posted the photo of Aiden's dad with a fan under the pub sign, calling him the Crocodile Drunk. As much as it hurt, Aiden had become obsessed reading all the comments until his mom had taken his phone and computer away.

I hope it lived.

"I wish you would have lived instead," said Aiden.

Me too, Bud. Me too. But at least one of us survived.

Aiden swore he could hear his dad laughing. He

shook his head, and he laughed a little too. It felt okay to laugh and not cry. Then he saw his mother coming with a water jug. She gave him a funny look when she saw the smile on his face. She poured water into the vase of flowers.

"You ready to go?" she asked, putting her arm around him.

"Do you want to talk to him?" he asked her. "I can go back to the car. But FYI, he's being Dad."

She lifted one eyebrow. "What does that mean?"

"You know — Dad. Always the joker."

"Typical. What was he joking about?"

Stays in the dressing room, Bud.

"Nothing, really. Just Dad stuff," said Aiden.

She shook her head. "Sometimes when I'm here, he says the funniest things. He can still make me laugh."

Aiden linked his arm through his mother's. "Let's go home," he said.

CHAPTER NINETEEN

TEAM NAME

The Saturday morning sun dawned to a blue sky and crisp fall air. Aiden jumped out of bed and threw his duvet on the floor. Getting up had never been so easy. He ran downstairs, where his mother was making coffee and something else that smelled amazing.

"French toast!" said Aiden.

"Breakfast of champions," she said. "And a healthy smoothie." The blender whirled, turning a banana, yogourt and frozen fruit into liquid. His mom poured the smoothie into a glass and handed it to him.

"Thanks," he said.

"You ready to rumble?" Aiden's mom did a little dance as she spoke.

"Mom, come on. That is so embarrassing. And be quiet at the game today, okay? You can cheer, but don't yell."

"Okay, okay. I've been to a lot of hockey games, you know. I do know the game. Hey, listen, I hope Grandpa can come today. I'm trying to get him there."

"I hope he can too."

"Oh, and I sewed your name bars on your jerseys and hung them in your closet."

"Thanks."

She winked at him. "Love the 'C.'"

Suddenly the smoothie felt like it had dropped from a seven-storey building to the bottom of Aiden's stomach. *What was he going to say to the team? How was he going to say it?*

Grandpa shuffled into the kitchen, dressed in his plaid housecoat and moccasin slippers.

"Morning, Dad," said Aiden's mom.

"Morning to you too." Grandpa plunked down in his seat.

Aiden poured his grandpa a cup of coffee and set the mug in front of him. "Mom said you might come to my game today."

"Of course," his grandpa said.

"I have to say something to my team today because I'm the captain."

"Say good luck and play hard, then get on the ice and do your best."

"Okay. Thanks, Grandpa." *That sounded like it came from a coaching manual.*

All morning Aiden thought about what he should say. He even practised up in his room, in front of the mirror. None of it paid off, though, because when he got into the car to go to the game, he was almost in a nervous lather. His leg shook more than ever, and he couldn't stop scratching his dress pants.

"Watch you don't put a hole in your new pants," said his mother.

They'd had to go get Aiden a new game-day suit because he'd grown out of his old one during the summer. Plus, that was the suit he'd worn to his dad's funerals, and he didn't want to wear it ever again.

He forced himself to stop scratching and clasped his hands together.

"Are you okay?" his mother asked.

"I'm fine."

"You sure?"

"Stop asking. I'm just nervous." He still hadn't told her about his meltdown before the pizza party.

"Okay. But you can talk to me, you know?"

"I know. Just let me be nervous."

It seemed to take forever to drive the three blocks to the arena. When his mom pulled up to the front doors, Aiden jumped out of the car as soon as it stopped.

"Good luck," she said.

"Skate hard," said Grandpa.

"Thanks," said Aiden. He yanked his equipment out of the trunk and headed into the arena. Coach Ira and

Coach Ben were standing by the door, also wearing suits. Both looked new. Coach Ira's hair was still a wild mess, but Coach Ben had slicked his back.

"Looking good," they said to Aiden.

"Same to you."

"Grad suits bought early," said Coach Ira. "You ready to play?"

"Totally," said Aiden.

Although Aiden thought he was going to be first in the dressing room, he wasn't. Manny was already there, taping his stick.

"Hey," said Aiden.

"Hey," replied Manny. "I'm here early to pick our team name." He kept taping, but he wasn't doing a very good job.

"Do you want me to help you?" Aiden asked.

"I think I'm supposed to do it this way. I looked it up online, and now I've completely forgotten. I'm too nervous to remember."

Aiden went over and sat beside Manny. Manny handed him the roll of black tape. Aiden had watched his dad so many times that for him it was like riding a bike. He tried to slow down how he wrapped the tape around the stick so Manny could learn.

When he finished, he said, "Nice and clean. You're ready for a tape-to-tape pass."

"Wow, thanks," Manny said.

Aiden moved over to his seat. He sat in the same place for every practice and now every game. "How do you like playing D?" he asked Manny.

"It's so awesome! I feel like I can see everything. Like it's more a game of chess now instead of a horse race."

"Good. You're doing great back there."

"You think so?"

"Yeah, I do." Aiden smiled.

Jory was the next one into the dressing room, and he took his place beside Aiden. Soon the room was filled. Not one person was missing, and everyone had come early. Craig had moved from his usual spot to sit between Bilal and Colin. A little bit of talking took place as everyone dressed, but not as much as usual. Aiden figured they were all nervous, especially since they were playing Peace Creek, who were known as a tough team.

Once everyone was dressed, Coach Ira and Coach Ben brought Susie and Audrey in.

"First game, team!" said Coach Ira. "I know we can do this. I want to see a good work ethic out there. Skate hard to every puck. But let's also try to get into the open, make room to get the puck. Always crash that net too. Garbage goals are goals — they still go on the scoreboard. Remember how we practised cycling, and try to use what we learned in practice to make some quick, clean passes. Tape-to-tape. Tree, you'll start in net. Audrey, you'll play the second half. All lines will get equal playing time, unless there is a power play. Power play will be rewarded for work ethic on the ice. Any questions?"

No one spoke.

"Okay, if there aren't any questions, let's gather around and have a cheer."

"We still don't have a name," said Manny.

"Right!" said Coach Ira.

"How about Chaos?" said Craig, with a smirk. "That's what we are. The most chaotic team ever."

Coach Ira frowned. "I'm not sure that works, O'Brien."

"I think it does," Craig snapped back.

"O'Brien, can it," said Jory.

"Why don't you shut your piehole."

Colin and Bilal snickered.

Aiden had to speak up. His throat was dry, and it felt like a ball was lodged in it. But he had to.

Say something, Bud. Aiden could hear his dad's voice in his mind.

He stood up and blurted out. "Great name! Hands in the middle, team. Let's go, Chaos!" *Oh god. Why did he say something so terrible?*

"Uh, Flor-i-dian, I was, uh, kidding," said Craig. "My dad said this whole organization is in chaos.

Maybe every team should be called Chaos, make it universal for Prairie Field."

Aiden wanted to crawl into a hole.

It's a good name, Bud. Be chaos on the ice.

"Let's go out and be chaos on the ice," said Aiden, not even knowing where the words were coming from. This was not what he had practised.

Silence.

He'd blown it. He had to say something else, to fix this.

You know what to do, Bud: Wreak havoc. Destroy teams. Win games.

Aiden repeated what his dad was saying in his head. "Wreak havoc. Destroy teams. Win games." Then he added more of his own words to the end. "Make chaos!" It was like his brain was connected directly to his mouth and he had no control.

"I like it," said Coach Ira. "Let's do it."

The team all put their hands in the middle. "Let's go, Chaos!"

They filed out and took to the ice. Susie skated beside Aiden during warm-up. "Good job," she said.

"You think so?" Aiden asked. "That was like babble city."

"I do. You done good, Captain," she said.

Craig's line was out first. They lined up, and the

referee dropped the puck. Craig shot it between the legs of the opposing centre, then wheeled around him. The player had no chance. Before he had even turned around, Craig was speeding toward the net. Jory was open on the right. He tapped his stick, but Craig deked around Peace Creek's defence and rifled a shot that hit the back of the netting. First shot on net. Craig alone had been chaos on the ice.

"He's so good," said J.J.

Aiden nodded. There was no way Craig should have been put on team three. He could have easily played on team one. Coach Ira didn't call the line in because they'd only been out for fifteen seconds. Craig totally dominated the next shift as well, but Peace Creek managed to stop him from getting another goal.

When the next whistle blew, Aiden, Susie and J.J.'s line took to the ice, with Colin and Manny heading out on defence. Jory skated by Aiden on his way to the bench, his head down.

Aiden patted Jory's shin pads with his stick. "Great skating," he said.

"Yeah, thanks," said Jory.

Because they were facing off in their offensive zone, Aiden spoke to his defence. "I'm going to try to get it back off the faceoff," he told them.

"I'll be ready," said Colin.

"Me too," said Manny.

Aiden tapped their backs and took his position at the faceoff circle.

He wrapped his hand around the bottom of his stick and stared at the puck. The referee dropped it, and Aiden quickly got it on his stick, sending it backwards. It was a soft pass, and Manny didn't move far enough forward to get the puck. Colin moved in and tried to get it, but it went out past the blueline. Aiden spun and skated out so they wouldn't be offside.

Colin carried the puck back in, and Aiden saw Susie move to cover the blueline, so he raced to the front of the net. J.J. skated forward without falling once. Colin circled around the back of the net, and Aiden moved out to the side, tapping his stick. Colin dished him a nice little pass, and Aiden had an opening at the front of the net. Two Peace Creek players swooped in on him, but then he saw J.J. alone by the hash marks. He passed the puck over to J.J., who swiped at it. The puck hit the crossbar as J.J. fell to the ice. Aiden saw the rebound and smacked at the puck. It went to the back of the net as J.J. was scrambling up. Aiden put his arms in the air and gave J.J. a hug.

"Did I get an assist?" J.J. asked.

"You sure did," said Aiden.

"Great work," said Susie.

"Good cover," said Colin to Susie.

They skated toward the bench, all smiles. Their smiles dropped when they saw Mr. O'Brien leaning over the glass behind the players' bench, talking at the coaches. "You should be double shifting my boy," he said.

"We have a game plan," said Coach Ira. "Line three, you're out."

Deke, Jacob and Henry took to the ice.

Jacob won the faceoff but lost the puck as he tried to stickhandle down the ice. The race was on as Peace Creek pushed forward with a three-on-two. Aiden stood to watch.

Deke dove to stop a Peace Creek player who was stickhandling, and sent him flying. The whistle blew. The ref made the tripping motion, and Deke skated to the penalty box.

"They just got out there," said Coach Ira. "We'll let them play a little longer."

"You're kidding me," said Craig. "We're on a penalty kill. I should be on both special teams."

Aiden looked behind him and was glad Mr. O'Brien wasn't at the glass anymore.

In the first thirty seconds of the Peace Creek power play, Tree had to make two spectacular saves. Then Coach Ira rolled the lines, and Craig got out for some penalty-kill time. The seconds slowly ticked down on the

Peace Creek power play until the teams were finally even strength.

Deke skated to the bench. "Sorry about that," he said.

"You dove," said Coach Ira. "I liked the energy."

Then it was Aiden's line's turn. At the end of his shift, Aiden got the puck and started hustling down the ice. He saw Susie cutting across and nailed her a pass. She took two strides and headed to the net. J.J. was with her. A Peace Creek stick went under her skate, and Susie went crashing into the boards.

Aiden skated over to her. "You okay?" he asked.

She looked up, grinning. "Did they get a penalty?"

Aiden glanced at the ref and saw him making the tripping motion. "Yup," he said.

"Then I'm all right." She got up and dusted off her legs. Their line skated toward the bench, where Craig was at it again.

"We need a power-play line out there."

"Line three out," said Coach Ira. "Short shift."

Aiden took his turn on the bench while Craig fumed.

"This guy doesn't know what he's doing," Craig said.

"We're up by two goals," said Aiden.

Thirty seconds ticked off the clock. Peace Creek got a chance to score a short-handed goal on Tree, but he covered the puck.

Coach Ira looked up and down the bench. "Okay, Craig, Jory, Aiden, out you go. Aiden, play left wing."

"Finally," said Craig.

Craig won the faceoff in a smooth sweep, then sent the puck to Aiden. Aiden saw Craig breaking away, so he flipped him a saucer pass. Without breaking stride, Craig picked up the puck and sailed down the ice. Aiden and Jory followed. Aiden got open on one side and Jory on the other as Peace Creek's defence attacked Craig. He could have easily passed, but he sniped a shot low and hard at the goalie.

The red light shone.

Aiden congratulated him, and Jory did too, but it was half-hearted.

On the bench, Jory whispered to Aiden, "I've touched the puck three times. That's it. Being on the first line is great, but not if you don't touch the puck."

"I know," said Aiden. "Even Connor McDavid gets more assists than goals. He always passes the puck."

When the final buzzer sounded to end the game, Aiden's team had won 3–0. While Aiden was thrilled with a win, he knew there was a lot of work to do to make the team a team.

CHAPTER TWENTY

HELPING NED

After the game, Aiden made sure he was the last person out of the dressing room. Different groups were starting to form, and Aiden didn't want it to seem like he was part of a particular one — least of all Craig's. Craig had Colin and Bilal following him around and laughing hysterically at whatever he said. Aiden had no idea what was so funny. It was like it was some big secret.

As Aiden was picking up his bag to leave, someone knocked on the door.

"Everyone decent?" a man called out.

"Yes," said Aiden.

A man wearing a blue turban that matched the team colour came into the dressing room. "Hello," he said. "I'm Jujhar's dad, Mr. Johar. I'm here to get the jerseys."

"I'm Aiden. Aiden Mallory." He held out his hand. "Pleased to meet you."

"Oh," Mr. Johar said. "You're the one who scored two goals?"

"No," said Aiden. "That's wasn't me."

"But you're the captain?"

"I am," replied Aiden.

"Well, good job today. J.J. is so happy being on this team. He started hockey when he was five and played for two years, then quit. Last year he decided to try again, and it was okay. But this year he's just loving it."

"I'm glad to hear that."

"He says you're a good leader."

"Thank you for telling me that." Aiden smiled. "I better go. My mom will be waiting for me — and my grandpa."

Mr. Johar gave Aiden a huge smile. "I sat with him today. He's a wealth of hockey knowledge."

"Yeah, he is," said Aiden.

Aiden walked out, leaving Mr. Johar to pick up the jerseys. He was going down the hall when he suddenly heard Ned, and it sounded like he was upset. Aiden dropped his equipment on the floor and took off at a sprint. He headed into the Zamboni area, and that's when he saw it. The floor was covered with the contents of a green garbage bag — french fries, food wrappers, paper cups, coffee grounds — and so many banana peels.

"Who did this? Why would someone do this?" Ned was talking loudly, staring at the trash, shaking his head. "It's so . . . disrespectful. I hate garbage! Don't they know how much banana peels make everything smell?"

"Ned . . . ?" said Aiden.

When Ned looked at Aiden, his eyes were glassy. Aiden understood what was happening to him even though their reasons for having meltdowns were different. "Ned, it's okay," said Aiden. "I'll help you clean it up."

"I can't stand banana peels. I can't stand . . . people doing this to the arena." Ned was visibly shaking. "I can't stand it, Aiden. It makes me . . . upset."

Then Aiden heard the laughing. He pivoted to see Craig, Bilal and Colin. Craig was in hysterics, and Colin and Bilal were laughing too, but less enthusiastically. They kept glancing at Craig like they were nervous.

"They're just banana peels," Craig said. Aiden was getting tired of that sickly sweet voice he used.

"This isn't funny!" Ned yelled this time.

"Ned. It's okay," said Aiden.

"No! No! No! It's . . . wrong!" Ned seemed to be struggling to breathe.

Aiden remembered when Ned had helped him. He gently put his hand on Ned's back. "It's okay, Ned," he said softly. "Just breathe. In and out. I'm here with you."

Aiden could see Ned's chest slowing down, which was good. But he could also hear Craig laughing, which was bad.

This is when you stand up to guys on your team, Bud.

Aiden might have hesitated to speak in the dressing room, but he couldn't over something like this. "Do you honestly think this is funny?" Aiden glared at Craig. "Why would you do something like this? You know it bothers him."

Craig kept laughing, but Bilal hung his head.

"This is so mean," said Aiden. "What did he ever do to you?"

"Why do people do things like this? It's awful. It's . . . immature." Ned's voice shook. His body trembled like he was freezing. "Don't they know the arena is a place to . . . respect? That's what it is. A place to . . . respect."

"Ned, I'll help you clean it up," said Aiden.

"He shouldn't freak out like this," said Craig. "It really is just banana peels and a bit of garbage."

Aiden spun around. "He can't help it. It's who he is, the way his brain works. Why? Why would you do this? It hurts him! It's just mean to do something like this, to someone who's only ever tried to help us. Get out of here, O'Brien."

There was a flicker of something in Craig's eyes, remorse perhaps, before it was covered over and his hardened and cocky act returned. "You can't prove we did anything to him."

"Whatever," said Aiden. "You know you did it, and I know it too. So, I hope you feel like crap."

Craig lowered his head. "I better go find my dad," he said.

After Craig had left, Colin stood there, running his hand through his hair. "I'm sorry, Ned," Colin said, his voice cracking. "I wasn't thinking."

"Me either," said Bilal. He looked close to tears. "It wasn't nice. Not at all. I'm really sorry."

Ned continued talking about respect and banana peels and garbage. His hands shook, and Aiden could see he was working on inhaling and exhaling. Then he finally glanced at Bilal and Colin and sadly shook his head.

"I'll help you clean up," Colin said to Aiden.

"Me too," said Bilal.

"Ned, we're going to clean this up. Okay?" said Aiden.

"Okay. Okay."

Aiden put his arm around Ned. "Why don't you go to the lobby and talk to my grandpa?" he said. "He came to the game today."

"I . . . thought I saw him." Ned looked at Aiden.

"Yeah. I know he wanted to talk to you after the game."

"What about?"

"Hockey. He wants to hear what you have to say."

"What about the . . . mess?"

"We'll take care of it." Aiden patted Ned's shoulder. "Don't worry."

"Yeah," said Bilal. "We'll get it done, Ned. We promise."

With Bilal and Colin's help, Aiden cleaned up the trash. The banana peels were disgusting — slimy and gross. He didn't speak to Bilal or Colin the entire time. When they were done, Aiden shook his gross hands.

"I'm going to go wash my hands," he said.

"I'm really sorry," said Bilal, his voice shaking. "I know what it's like to be on that end of things."

"Me too," said Colin.

Aiden nodded. "Maybe remember that next time. It's not fair to treat him or *anyone* like that. See you at practice."

After washing his hands, Aiden picked up his bag that he'd dropped in the hallway, then headed to the lobby. The first thing he saw was Ned standing with his grandpa. He walked over to them.

"Hi, Grandpa," said Aiden. "Did you enjoy the game?"

His grandpa nodded.

Ned just stood there with his hands in his pockets. Aiden glanced around, and no one was in earshot except Grandpa, who didn't seem to be listening right now. Aiden turned to Ned.

"All cleaned up," Aiden said quietly.

"Thanks." Ned shook his head back and forth. "I don't like that boy. He's . . . disrespectful like his daddy."

Aiden desperately wanted to cheer Ned up, so he changed the subject. "My backhand is improving because of you."

Ned nodded. "Gotta keep practising."

"I like being on the ice with you, Ned." Aiden smiled to make Ned smile. "You help me so much."

"Let's go out again," said Ned. "I'm always up early. And you work hard. I like that. I like helping you. To me that's . . . fun."

Aiden had been worried about whoever was knocking at the arena door the other morning, but it was probably just nothing anyway. At least, that's what he told himself.

"Okay," said Aiden. Then he grinned. "Maybe if I keep practising with you, I'll score a Ned Backhand Goal in a game."

"You're naming a goal after me?"

"You bet."

"Monday morning," Ned said, and he smiled.

CHAPTER TWENTY—ONE

GAME TWO

On Monday Craig didn't show up at school until eleven, when he walked into the classroom with wet hair. Mr. Rowland gave his head a little shake but kept talking about the Egyptian pyramids.

"Lucky dude," whispered Jory. "I'd do anything to get out of this."

"Me too," Aiden whispered back, then yawned. He'd had his practice with Ned at six a.m., then had to pull himself back out of bed to make the bus. Craig got to practise, sleep in, and miss school.

For the rest of the morning, Aiden doodled on his notebook, only half-listening. All he wanted to do was play ball hockey at lunch to wake up.

Once he was outside with his plastic stick, Aiden stood back, letting the older boys make the teams. When he saw he was on a team with Craig, he groaned. The last person he wanted to be with was O'Brien, especially after what he did to Ned, but at least he wouldn't get shoved to the concrete again.

"Come on," said Craig. "Let's do some damage."

Aiden ignored him, refusing to make eye contact. The game started, and Aiden spent the first few minutes just running up and down, not touching the rolling ball. Then he nabbed it from a player on the other team and took off toward the net. Beside him Craig called out, "I'm open."

Aiden automatically fired off a pass that landed on Craig's stick. He blasted it home.

"Great pass." Craig patted him on the back.

Aiden shrugged his hand off.

By the time the bell went, Aiden and Craig had combined for four goals. Faces flushed, Aiden walked back to the school with Jory.

Craig ran up behind them. "We should ask Coach to put us on a line together again," he said to Aiden.

Aiden didn't want to start talking to Coach Ira about being on a different line. "I think Coach is trying to balance the lines. So far he's done a pretty good job. We're undefeated, you know."

Craig laughed. "We've only played one game!"

"I can't wait to play this weekend," said Jory.

"Me too," said Craig. "My dad made me skate so hard this morning. He brought this friend of his, a coach from another town. He made me shoot and shoot."

"Yeah, I had to . . ." Aiden's words trailed off. In trying to equal Craig, Aiden had almost blabbed about him and Ned.

"What were you going to say?" Craig asked Aiden.

"Nothing. Just that I made myself practise on my net outside the other day."

Craig squinted at him.

"Don't believe me then," snapped Aiden. "Come over and I'll prove it."

Craig's face changed. "Really? I can come to your house?"

Uh-oh. Aiden didn't think Craig would ever want to come to his house. It would be so awkward to have him over. Especially after what Craig had done to Ned. Aiden didn't know how to answer.

As if reading his thoughts, Craig said, "I didn't mean to hurt Ned, you know. I didn't think banana peels would be that bad."

"They are to him," said Aiden.

"Yeah, I guess so. I can tell him I'm sorry."

"You should," said Aiden.

"Sure." Craig paused for a second, then said, "Hey, my dad has more ice next week. You could come with us." He nudged Aiden with his shoulder. "You'd miss school."

"I don't think my mom would let me," said Aiden.

"Too bad. Extra practice could really help your game."

If only he knew.

* * *

Aiden woke up on Saturday morning thinking about his snap shot and backhand and everything else Ned had gone over with him in their practices that week. He felt ready for today's game. It was an away game in Barr River, a town smaller than Prairie Field and a good forty-five minutes away. Chaos didn't play until three, so he had some time to practise what he was going to say to the team in the dressing room. Still wearing his pyjamas, he stood in front of his bedroom mirror and tried to talk.

"This is it, guys. Game day." *That sounded so awful.*

Aiden tried again. "Barr River is fast and hard hitting, but let's stay on our game. Let's be the hardest working team on the ice."

"Aiden!" his mother called from downstairs. "Breakfast."

"Coming." Aiden was happy that he got to eat instead of talk to a stupid mirror.

Downstairs, Grandpa was already at the table, slurping his coffee and spilling it on the placemat.

"Morning, Grandpa."

He lifted his hand to wave at Aiden.

"Eggs?" Aiden asked.

"I thought you could use some protein," said his mom.

"You have a game today?" Grandpa asked.

"Yeah," said Aiden. "I want to say something good to the team. You know, as captain."

Grandpa nodded. "Always play your own game. Play as a team. Every person has a role and is part of the team."

"Wow," said Aiden. "That's way better than what I was practising."

"And make eye contact."

"What?"

"Look your teammates in the eyes, Luke."

Aiden smiled a small smile. "I will. Thanks, Grandpa."

* * *

Aiden stood in front of his teammates. He had asked Coach Ira for a few minutes to speak to everyone without the coaches in the room — just the players. He sucked in a deep breath. *He could do this. He could.* His legs were shaking. His heart was racing. His entire body was sweating like a tap on full blast. But Aiden knew nothing was happening in a meltdown kind of way. It was just nerves.

"We're a team," he said. He hoped his voice wasn't high and squeaky. He looked around the room and tried to make eye contact, just like Grandpa had said. "Let's play like a team and respect everyone on our team." He stopped, but that made him realize everyone was staring at him. *What else had Grandpa said?*

What else had Grandpa said? Think!

"Um, everyone has a role and that's what makes a team. Together we can beat Barr River!"

Tree started tapping his stick on the floor. Colin joined in, and so did Bilal and Manny and Jory and soon the entire team, even Craig. Something swelled inside of Aiden. "Let's do our cheer."

When everyone's hand was in the middle, Aiden started the cheer. "One, two, three!"

"Let's go, Chaos!"

Everyone filed out to the ice, where the coaches were waiting for them. Coach Ira patted Aiden's helmet. "We heard the cheer from here," he said.

The game started with Aiden, still playing second-line centre, on the bench. The play went up and down the ice a few times without a whistle. Then Craig got the puck, and he raced through the neutral zone toward Barr River's net. His speed was just too much for anyone on the Barr River team, and when he got over the blueline and in front of their defence, he broke around it like the opposing players were pylons. Jory had wheeled down the ice as well and was wide open in the slot. He kept tapping his stick. Aiden watched as Craig looked over at Jory — then he passed!

Jory one-timed it, and the puck flew to the back of the net.

"What a play!" said Aiden.

When Craig came off the ice, Coach Ira gave him a huge pat on the back. "That's teamwork," he said. "Beautiful pass."

Craig was smiling underneath his cage. Jory too. Aiden slapped both their hands. "Great start," he said.

Jory whispered to Aiden, "It's always great when O'Brien's dad has to work on game day. O.B. passes the puck. Plus, your pre-game talk helped." He nudged Aiden with his shoulder.

Aiden glanced around the strange arena. Sure enough, he didn't see Mr. O'Brien. And come to think of it, Jory and Craig had come in the dressing room together.

"Aiden's line, you're out," said Coach Ira. "Manny, Colin, you're on D."

"Go get 'em!" said Craig.

Aiden, Susie and J.J. took to the ice. Right off the faceoff, Barr River was aggressive. The puck skidded around with no team taking real possession. Then one of the Barr River forwards slapped it up the ice and it became loose. Manny chased it down and picked it up. He went around the back of the net and stopped, stick-handling and looking around. Seeing Susie on the wing, he fired it around to her. She picked it up and hugged the boards. Aiden skated with her, but the biggest player on Barr River pinned her along the boards so there was no way she could pass. Aiden rushed in to support her.

The Barr River player shoved Susie, and she went flying to the ice. The ref's arm went up and the whistle blew.

Aiden skated over to Susie as she was getting up and brushing the snow off her socks. Now it was her turn to grin under her cage. "We're going to power play," she said.

Aiden grinned back at Susie. She drew penalties every game. They both skated toward the bench, but Coach Ira motioned for Aiden to stay out just as Craig and Jory skated onto the ice.

"I'll get the puck off the faceoff," said Craig, "and send it back." He glared at Manny. "Be ready."

Manny nodded.

Sure enough, when the puck dropped, Craig took full control, sending it back to Manny. Manny immediately sent it across the ice. Aiden kept his feet moving and headed over to the boards. Colin picked up the puck and sent it down to him.

Aiden heard Ned's voice in his head: Look before you get the puck. Then pass quick. Pass quick.

Aiden saw Craig moving, feet shuffling, trying to get open. Jory was behind the net. If Aiden got the puck to him, he could get it to Craig. Aiden rifled off the pass. Jory picked it up and sent it to Craig. Aiden moved in for a rebound. Craig sniped and hit the post, the ping echoing through the arena. Aiden scooted to the puck and picked it up, seeing Craig on the other side. He dished off a quick pass and Craig fired it top shelf. Goal!

Aiden threw his arms in the air, then skated over to Craig. "Great shot," he said.

"Tic-tac-toe," said Craig. "Told you we should be on a line together."

"Yup. Tic-tac-toe."

They skated to the bench with Craig leading the charge for high-fives.

The game ended with a 5–1 score. Aiden had picked up another assist on a goal that J.J. managed to sneak in on a rebound. Susie and Jory had each scored one, and Craig filled in the other two, getting four points total.

The noise in the dressing room after the game was awesome! Aiden couldn't stop smiling. They'd won their second game, and everyone was happy.

Coach Ira brought Susie and Audrey in when everyone was finally clothed. "Listen up," he said. The room stilled.

"Just a few things before you go. We only have one practice next week, so I want everyone there early and prepared. It's important that we make the most of our time. The tournament is coming up in two weeks, and we need to focus and use every minute of our ice time. I've received all the information about the tournament. There are four teams in our pool, and it will be a weekend of three round robin games, a semi and a final."

"We need extra ice for this," said Craig. "I know there's some ice in Smith Pond. It's not the best arena, but it's still ice."

Coach Ira nodded. "Okay, so about that. I talked to the parents, and there are a few opposed to buying extra ice, so once the outdoor rink is ready, we will pick up extra time outside. It won't be long now."

"Parents don't want to pay a little extra?" Craig shook his head. "We have a tournament coming up! The outdoor ice won't be ready before then."

"It is what it is," said Coach Ira. "See you on Thursday evening. Practice is at five thirty, so don't be late. We have to use our time well."

Once Coach Ira had left, Aiden zipped up his bag and started to put on his jacket.

"Whose parents won't pay?" Craig barked.

"My mom can't," said Manny.

"Are you kidding me?" Craig rolled his eyes at Manny. "You're going to wreck our winning streak, you know. If we lose the tournament, it's your fault."

"My fault?" Manny sounded like he might cry.

Oh no. Aiden had to think fast. Really fast.

Aiden stood up. "It won't be Manny's fault. Maybe we just need to think of some way to raise money to pay for extra ice time. What if . . . what if . . . we did some sort of fundraising?"

"And do what? Sell Girl Guide cookies?" Craig shook his head.

"Not Girl Guide cookies," piped up Susie. "But we *could* have a bake sale. Aiden's mom could make cupcakes. We'd make so much money! We could sell each cupcake for a dollar — or even two dollars. If we all brought some sort of baking, we could probably make a couple hundred dollars."

Susie looked at Aiden. "How many cupcakes can your mom make?"

Aiden shrugged. "Five dozen? Six dozen?" *Was his mom going to kill him for saying that? She said she would help.*

"That's seventy-two dollars right there, if she does six dozen and we only charge a dollar," said Susie. "How much does ice cost?"

"Over a hundred an hour," said Craig.

"Then we charge two dollars," said Susie. "Or even three."

My mom could make chocolate-chip cookies," said Manny. "And gingersnaps."

"Well, my mother doesn't bake," snarled Craig. He stood up.

Manny glanced over at Craig. "My mom could make enough for both of us," he said.

For once, Craig didn't have a comeback for Manny.

CHAPTER TWENTY-TWO

UNSELFISH PLAYS

On the way home Aiden's mother kept glancing over at him. Aiden knew she was waiting for him to talk. She'd already done her "good game" stuff and her game analysis, and now there was silence in the car.

Finally Aiden said, "I think I did a good job being captain today."

"Oh, honey, that's so nice to hear. What makes you think that?"

"I dunno. I talked to the team before the game and looked everyone in the eyes like Grandpa told me to do. I think I got them fired up. Craig even passed the puck. But his dad wasn't there, and Jory said he plays better when his dad isn't around."

"Yes, he made some really unselfish plays today."

"Oh, and we're having a bake sale to make money to buy extra ice," said Aiden. "You have to make cupcakes. We just have to figure out when to have it."

"Is that so? What if I said no to the baking?"

Wide-eyed, Aiden looked at his mother. "You have to. I'm the captain. Everyone *loves* your cupcakes."

She started laughing. "Chocolate or vanilla?"

Aiden frowned at her. "Duh. Both."

"Don't you dare duh me," she said, shaking her head. "I'll make cupcakes but you're helping me bake — and that's non-negotiable."

"Deal," said Aiden.

* * *

At exactly six o'clock Wednesday morning, Aiden had his skates laced and was on the ice, his blades cutting through the clean sheet. These mornings were just routine now, and no matter how early they started, he looked forward to his time with Ned. Here he could forget everything and just get better. He still needed to improve on the ice to be the captain he wanted to be.

Aiden took shot after shot until he was soaked with sweat.

"Wow," said Ned. "That's some good target practice. You're getting it, kid."

"Thanks. You've helped me so much." Aiden paused. "I even got two assists last game."

"I heard about that. You know what else? That team-mate of yours said he was sorry."

Aiden looked at Ned. "He did?"

"Yup. I'm sure it's because of you too." Ned winked. "Outdoor ice will be ready soon. No one goes out in the morning, so we can . . . practise whenever we want. I can only do mornings. I like to watch hockey at night. Every single stinking game I can. Lots of . . . maintenance to do to get the ice going outside, but I get it done. Every year. Maybe you can . . . help?"

Aiden was about to say yes when he heard a loud banging. "What's that?" he asked.

Ned looked up. "Pipes?"

The noise sounded again. Aiden saw Ned's face change to fear.

"Lights," Ned whispered.

"I'll get the net," said Aiden.

Ned had the lights off in seconds, and Aiden pushed the net to the side. His heart hammered under his sweatshirt. His sweat had gone cold and he started to shiver. He and Ned huddled behind a wall in the dark. Within seconds, the pounding on the door stopped. This hadn't happened since that one time a couple weeks back, and that seemed like ages ago. So much had happened since that day.

"What do you think that noise was?" Aiden whispered.

Ned shook his head over and over. "Don't know. But we gotta get out of here."

"Okay."

"We gotta go. We gotta go. " Ned kept shaking his head.

"You're right, Ned," said Aiden. "We'll both leave. And we won't turn on any more lights."

"No more practices either."

"Agreed," said Aiden.

Aiden ran home, his breath swirling in front of his face. The temperature had definitely dropped. Forget the indoor ice — they could go outside soon anyway. As Aiden got near his house, he saw a car idling out front, puffs of smoke coming from its exhaust.

Aiden quickly looked around for someplace to hide. *Where could he go?* Behind a telephone pole? There weren't a lot of trees in the Prairies. He looked at his neighbour's house with its one lone bush by the back porch. It didn't have leaves, but it had lots of branches.

He darted over and squatted down. *Was he hidden enough?* His body shivered, but he tried to hold still. He peered through the skinny branches, watching the car as it started to move slowly down the street as if the driver was looking for someone. Aiden's body shook. His legs cramped but he remained still. *What if they saw him?* He held his breath and watched the lights of the car turn into red tail lights as it crept forward. It finally got to the corner and turned down the street that led to the arena. Now was Aiden's chance to bolt.

He snuck around the back of his neighbour's house,

toward his own, staying out of the glow from the street lights. Once he was at his house, Aiden took one last look to make sure the car was gone. He crept in through the back door, tiptoed up the stairs, and dove under his covers.

* * *

"My dad has ice for me on Friday," Craig said to Aiden in the hallway before school started. "You wanna come?"

"Guaranteed my mom won't let me." Aiden couldn't look Craig in the eyes. Not this morning. He was still shaking from what had happened at the arena.

"You won't miss much at school. Plus, it'd be fun to have a friend with me. If you come, maybe we could get on a line together permanently. I'd get a ton of goals playing with you." Craig paused. "My dad can even be okay sometimes."

"It's not that," said Aiden. "I just know my mom will say no."

"Okay." Craig's shoulders seemed to sag.

"The outdoor ice is going to be ready soon," said Aiden. "We can skate on that. I bet Ned would come out in his goalie equipment."

"Ned? Are you kidding me?"

"He's, um, pretty good," said Aiden.

Craig eyed Aiden. "How do you know?"

Aiden sucked in a deep breath. *Why did he say that?*

Why did he even mention Ned? "Um, my dad used to go out with him. I guess Ned really helped him."

"Yeah, right. As if I believe that." Craig glanced at Aiden. "By the way, I apologized to him — to Ned."

"Good for you," said Aiden.

"Hey, wait up!" Susie called from behind them.

Aiden turned and sighed with relief. With Susie joining them, he could get away from talking to Craig about Ned, and ice time, and extra practice.

She ran toward them holding a stack of papers. "I made posters for the bake sale."

Aiden stopped to look at what she'd done.

"Wow," he said. "These are great!"

"You just wait," said Susie. "I'm going to put these up all around town. And I got a bakery downtown to donate cookies because I can't bake. I tried yesterday and my cookies were as flat as pancakes, so I showed the bakery and they laughed and said they would love to help our cause."

"That's what we are, all right," said Craig. "A cause."

"Great job, Susie!" Aiden held up his fist, and she bumped it.

"The tournament is going to be so much fun," said Susie. "I'm going to do a sign-up sheet so everyone on our team can take a shift selling."

"Perfect," said Aiden. Susie had offered to phone

Mr. Ramos to ask when the team could have their bake sale. He wanted them to do it on the Friday night of the tournament and said they could keep the money from the sale for their own ice time, instead of having it go toward the lights. It meant they wouldn't get any extra ice time before the tournament, but they might make enough money for two ice times down the road — maybe even to help get them ready for provincials.

"So many people are talking about the tournament," said Susie, her voice brimming with excitement. "They were so pumped at the bakery. And when I dropped off a poster at the hair salon, they said they donated a free haircut to the silent auction. I've heard the silent-auction table is incredible. They even have some new hockey equipment donated from the sports store. Woohoo!"

"My dad doesn't want me to take part in the bake sale," said Craig.

"Why not?" Susie asked.

"He thinks everyone should have just paid up so we wouldn't have to be doing all this work."

"What a stick in the mud," said Susie. "I think it's way more fair this way."

"Morning, students," said Mr. Rowland.

Mr. Rowland looked from Aiden to Craig to Susie. "You get a free pass to enter the room. Did you know that?"

"Monopoly gives two hundred dollars," said Craig.

Mr. Rowland did his one eyebrow up, one eyebrow down look.

Susie ignored Craig and handed Mr. Rowland one of her posters. "You should come, Mr. Rowland. Bring your kids. Aiden's mother makes the best cupcakes, but you will have to get there early or they will be sold out. Team Chaos is raising money for ice time, and the arena is raising money for new lights."

Mr. Rowland shook his head and laughed. "That was a good sales pitch, Susie."

"I know." She smiled and bounced into the room.

Aiden followed Susie in. The tournament was causing such energy in the town. Everyone was talking about it. Aiden desperately wanted to play well. Ned had been helping him so much, and he knew that he had improved. Despite that, a nagging feeling settled in Aiden's stomach.

Who had banged on the arena door?

* * *

Over the next few days, Aiden jumped whenever the phone rang, expecting the person on the other end to tell his mother he had snuck on the ice. He breathed a sigh of relief every time it was just someone from the tournament committee needing to ask his mom a question. The tournament hype was getting bigger and bigger, and Aiden's mom was busy helping with the silent auction. She'd donated a few of his dad's jerseys, and so much other stuff. Aiden had offered his signed Sidney Crosby photo as well. The dining-room table was starting to fill up with all of the items that had been donated.

Saturday was the last game before the tournament, and by then Aiden was feeling one hundred percent confident no one was going to nail him. Since he was off the hook about sneaking on the ice, he could concentrate on playing. They'd had an incredible practice on Thursday, and he was excited for this game — and he had finally started to feel excited about the tournament too.

Today's game was on home ice. Aiden warmed up, then took his place on the bench. On his first shift out, he managed to pick up a loose puck and started heading down the ice. He saw J.J. skating beside him and passed him the puck. J.J. sped down the ice without falling once, his legs stretching, his strides incredible. Once they were over the blueline, Aiden swung behind J.J. in a move they had practised on Thursday. J.J. sent the puck back to Aiden, who got ready. In a quick release, he flicked his wrist and blasted off a snap shot. The goalie got his glove hand up, but the puck sailed right past it and into the back of the net. J.J. rushed over to Aiden.

"Great shot!" J.J. said.

"Good play," Aiden replied.

Aiden skated over to the bench and went down the line, slapping the gloves of his teammates. When he got to the end, he saw Ned. Ned had a big smile on his face and was holding up his thumb.

"That's my . . . boy," he yelled.

Aiden gave him a wave before he headed to the faceoff circle for the rest of his shift.

After the game, which Chaos easily won, the team chatted non-stop about the bake sale and the tournament. Susie had the bake sale under complete control, and Aiden and Jory were letting her run with it and helping where she needed them.

Once he had dressed and the talk had died down, Aiden went out to the lobby, but he couldn't see his mother anywhere. He spotted Ned, who was grinning like crazy, so Aiden went over to him.

"You played one heck of a game. That was some snap shot. Wowee!" said Ned.

Aiden had picked up a goal and an assist. Of course, Craig had got two goals and an assist. On top of that, Jory had scored on a huge blast, and Susie on a sneaky goal.

"Thanks. I think target practice paid off." Aiden glanced around. "Have you seen my mom?"

"Oh, she's talking to Mr. O'Brien."

"Seriously?" *Why would she be talking to Craig's dad?* Were they discussing the extra ice time Mr. O'Brien got for Craig? Aiden wondered if maybe his mother would let him miss school after all.

"Do you know where they are?" Aiden asked.

"Upstairs in the . . . office," said Ned.

"The office? That's weird, but hey, thanks." Aiden picked up his bag and headed to find his mom. He dropped his bag at the bottom of the stairs, then took them two at a time.

He heard the voices before he got to the top.

CHAPTER TWENTY-THREE

CONSEQUENCES

"Aiden would never do that," said his mother.

"It was him," said Craig's dad. Aiden could recognize that angry voice anywhere.

"Len, you're making accusations without any evidence," said a third voice Aiden couldn't quite place.

"Why don't we just ask Aiden if you're that concerned?" his mother asked.

"Sure, let's ask. I'll bet he denies it," said Mr. O'Brien.

"It might not be that big of a deal, if it happened," said the third person. "Especially if it was only once." Aiden was now pretty sure this was Mr. Ramos, the president of the minor hockey association.

"It was more than once," said Mr. O'Brien. "And it is a big deal! I've been paying for my boy's ice, and your kid is sneaking on for free. Being in the arena with the lights on costs money, which this organization doesn't have. He should be suspended, and my son should be made the captain."

Aiden's heart started thwacking against his shirt. This was not good. Not good at all. *Suspended?* His stomach sank. *Would he not play the entire year? Would he not even get to play in his dad's memorial tournament?*

What had he done?

"Oh, so is that what it's really about?" Now Aiden's mother sounded mad. "Aiden was made captain, and you don't like it?"

"You think you're something because you married Luke and became a hockey wife? Well, look where you ended up."

"I can't believe you just said that. Why don't you shut up, Len! Just shut up." Aiden's mother was yelling now. Aiden had never heard her speak like that to anyone.

"Enough, you two. This isn't about your own battle," said Mr. Ramos.

"I'm sorry," said Aiden's mom. Aiden imagined her running her hands through her hair, the distress on her face. *She didn't deserve this because of what he had done.* He had to do something.

Aiden opened the door and slowly walked into the office.

"Hi," he squeaked.

"Aiden," said his mother. She gave him a look as if to ask, *What did you hear?*

"Let's ask him now," said Mr. O'Brien. He crossed his arms over his chest.

Mr. Ramos held up his hands. "Sure," he said, like

he just wanted the argument to end. "Aiden, Mr. O'Brien here thinks someone has been coming in early and using the ice when the arena is supposed to be closed. Was it you?"

Aiden sucked in a deep breath. He'd love to say no — he really would — but that would just be another lie. His best bet was to tell the truth, but his mouth was having a hard time working. The adults were staring at him, waiting for an answer.

He looked down at the floor, at the old, worn-out carpet. *What if he got suspended?* His heart felt as if it weighed a million pounds. His eyes filled with water, but he couldn't cry. He couldn't. Things were going so well for him now. He was finally being a good captain and improving his skills. *Why did he blow it?* He had just wanted to get better. How could that be such a bad thing?

"Aiden?" his mother asked.

Aiden lifted his head. He closed his eyes for a second to breathe and stop the tears. "Yes," he said.

Mr. Ramos eyed him. "More than once?"

Aiden looked back down at the faded carpet and nodded.

"Two, three, four times?" Mr. O'Brien barked out.

"Enough, Len," said Aiden's mother. "You don't need the exact amount."

"Did Ned let you in?" Mr. O'Brien asked.

Aiden jerked his head up. "It's not his fault." His words rushed out. "It's not his fault. I asked him to come out with me, to open the doors. I just wanted to practise and get better and be like my dad. Ned did nothing wrong."

"Oh, Aiden." His mother sighed.

"You should suspend him," said Mr. O'Brien. "The association took a vote. The arena was supposed to be closed Monday mornings and every Wednesday until it gets new lights. This is wrong. His suspension should come into effect before the tournament." Mr. O'Brien smirked.

"No!" cried Aiden. "It's named after my dad. I have to play in it."

Mr. O'Brien turned to Aiden's mother. "I **bought** ice time for my boy. Maybe you should have used some of that NHL salary to buy some for your kid."

Aiden's mother spoke up. "I think suspension is the wrong punishment. It's too harsh."

How could Mr. O'Brien want to punish him this way? Especially after all the damage *he'd* done and how he'd charged on the ice and yelled in the stands. And what about Craig and how he had treated Ned? Aiden knew enough not to say anything about that, though, and risk making it look like he was whining. Instead he just stood there, arms hanging at his sides and sweat dripping down the middle of his back. His heart ticked like a clock out of control.

Suspended?

Miss playing in his dad's memorial tournament?

He had to do something. He couldn't panic, he just couldn't. Suddenly he thought of how he had handled the dressing room when Craig was being nasty.

Speak.

"I have an idea," Aiden said quickly. His voice was high and squeaky.

All the adults stared at him. He had to continue. He stood tall. "I'm sorry. I really am. I just wanted some extra practice, but I understand now why it was wrong. Instead of a suspension," he said, "I could help Ned with the maintenance around the arena. I could even help maintain the outdoor rink when it's up and running. He said it's a lot of work."

Mr. Ramos looked at Aiden and nodded his head. "That's a good idea. The outdoor ice will be going in soon, and there's always a lot of watering and shovelling to do."

"Something should be done about Ned too," said Mr. O'Brien.

Aiden's heart sank. *Not Ned.* Working around the arena was his life, and if it wasn't for Aiden, none of this would have happened. Aiden shook his head, knowing he had to do something else.

"I'll take the suspension," he said. "Just please leave Ned out of this."

"Aiden," said his mother gently.

"Sounds good to me," said Mr. O'Brien.

"I'm not in agreement," said Mr. Ramos. "I think working around the arena, helping Ned, is a reasonable punishment."

"Okay," said Aiden quickly. "I'll start next week. I could work four hours a week—"

"No. He should be suspended, or at least be stripped of his 'C,'" said Mr. O'Brien, refusing to give up. "Those are the right consequences."

Aiden stared at him. Mr. O'Brien had his hands under his armpits and was tapping them. He had the same look on his face that Craig got when he was being mean.

"Either lose the 'C' or be suspended," Mr. O'Brien repeated. "That seems fair to me."

"No!" Aiden's mother spoke loudly. "That is not fair." Her face was all red and . . . uh-oh . . . were those blotches on her neck? Aiden had seen those same blotches that horrible afternoon when the phone rang, telling them his dad had died.

"Picking up trash doesn't cut it." Mr. O'Brien was firm. "Ned let the kid in, so why is he the one getting help here?"

"After all the things you've done over the years!" Aiden's mom almost shrieked.

Aiden closed his eyes for a second. This was horrible. *Was it worth all this?* Suddenly Aiden felt exhausted, deflated. Yes, he liked wearing the "C," but he'd rather play on his team and *not* have his mother break out in hives.

"I'll, um, give up the 'C,'" he said. "As long as Ned doesn't get in trouble for any of this."

"Aiden!" his mother spoke out. "This is not right."

"Mom, it's okay. I'd rather do that than get suspended. I want to play in Dad's tournament. Please. I have to."

"That settles it then. I'll tell the coaches," said Mr. O'Brien.

"No. You won't." Mr. Ramos spoke. He sounded as exhausted as Aiden felt. "I will, and if you do, I'll get *you* suspended."

Then Mr. Ramos turned to Aiden. "And you only have to work two hours a week."

* * *

That night Aiden's mother sat on the end of his bed.

"I can't believe you snuck out of the house at five thirty in the morning to go shoot pucks with Ned," she said. "You do know it was wrong?"

"Yeah, I do." Aiden was curled up in a ball, ready to go to sleep. It had been a painfully long day, and his emotions had taken charge like a bull going after a matador. Yup, he'd cried, but only in his room. His time as captain had been short-lived. Now it was at a dead stop. Done. Over.

His mother stroked his hair.

"Dad used to go on the ice with Ned too," he said.

"That was a long time ago," she said. "I bet your grandpa knew he was sneaking on the ice. He knew everything about what every player on his team was up to. He probably approved the extra practice." Then she paused and picked a piece of lint off his duvet cover. "But you can't do that now. They had the arena closed for a reason."

"I know, Mom. I'm sorry. I wasn't thinking."

"Did he help you? Ned?"

"Oh, yeah. He's pretty good in net. He made me do target practice."

"Target practice?"

"You're not as mad as I thought you would be." Aiden sat up a little and leaned against his headboard.

"I'm not happy, but I understand why you did it. The cost of running this arena is high right now, and it does need new lights, so I hope you know why it wasn't the right thing to do. And Len has been paying for his son to have extra ice time, so it wasn't fair to your teammates either. Still, he didn't need to be such a jerk."

"Craig is sometimes too. But then sometimes he's okay."

She pursed her lips and shook her head. "I'm still mad at Len for even *suggesting* that you give up being the captain. Your coach is not happy at all. It is so unfair, and I want to fight this. Working at the arena is enough punishment."

"Leave it alone, Mom. I talked to Coach Ira too," said Aiden. "He's going to announce a new captain at our practice on Monday afternoon. At least I can play in the tournament. That's what's important to me — to do that for Dad."

"Your coach is thinking this may only last a game or two."

"I hope so, but I know I won't have the 'C' for the tournament. And I'm sure Craig will tell everyone at school on Monday morning." The thought of going to school made Aiden's stomach sick.

"That will be tough," his mom said.

"Does that mean I can stay home?"

"Nice try." She tickled Aiden's ribs.

He yawned and lay back down, curling into a ball again and facing the wall. Suddenly the room went quiet. The silence hovered over Aiden, making his body feel heavy.

"Going on the ice like that, with Ned," he said. "I

don't know, it helped me get closer to Dad for some reason." He paused and stared at the wall. "I'm not one hundred percent sorry, you know. I think I'd give up that 'C' any day to be close to him again."

"Oh, Aiden. I'm so sorry that you're not going to get to know him like you should. It doesn't seem fair that you only had him for such a short time." She kissed the side of his head.

Aiden squeezed his eyes shut.

Sorry, Dad. I guess we both messed up.

CHAPTER TWENTY-FOUR

DRESSING-ROOM SPEECH

Aiden went to school on Monday dreading the day. He was positive Mr. O'Brien would have told Craig everything. But Craig wasn't there, so the first part of the morning went by without a word from anyone.

Instead of heading directly outside when the recess bell went, Aiden approached Mr. Rowland and handed him a new outline. "Um, could I change my essay topic?" he asked.

Mr. Rowland looked at Aiden over the rim of his glasses. "I marked the last one. You did fine. You should be writing the actual essay now."

"I know, but I don't like my topic anymore."

Mr. Rowland shook his head and sighed, but he took Aiden's paper anyway. "You realize you're making this a lot of work for both of us."

"Thanks," said Aiden. "I think this is going to be a way better topic."

"No hockey?" He eyed Aiden.

"A little. But it's way better, trust me."

As slowly as he could, Aiden got his winter coat on

and headed outside. The cold wind howled, and he pulled up his hood.

Susie ran over to him. "J.J.'s mom is making two *huge* batches of double-fudge brownies for the bake sale!" She did her circle dance as she held up two fingers. "Double batch. Double fudge. Double money."

Did she really not know about him losing the "C"?

They talked until the bell rang. As Aiden entered the school, Jory caught up to him. "I'm going to have that captains' party on Thursday night. My mom said we can have pizza. She'll pick us all up from school and drop you off too."

"Um, that sounds great," said Aiden. Although, that wouldn't happen for him anyway. Not after Jory found out. Aiden would no longer be invited to the captains' party because he wouldn't be a captain. *Had Craig kept his mouth shut?*

Behind Jory, Aiden suddenly saw Craig. His hair was wet again, which meant he probably had a personal ice session that morning. He gave Aiden an almost sad smile. It was weird. *Where was his usual sneer? Why wasn't he telling everyone that Aiden was no longer the captain?*

Aiden tried to keep himself beside Jory and away from Craig, but when Jory disappeared to the washroom, Aiden was left with Craig. Alone.

"Hey," said Aiden.

"I don't agree with my dad," said Craig.

So he did know.

"It's over," said Aiden.

"And I told him so," said Craig. "You *should* be our captain. I think you might be one of the best captains I've had."

Aiden squinted at Craig. *Was he being serious? Or was this a joke?* But he honestly looked serious.

"Um, thanks," said Aiden.

"My dad didn't like it much when I told him you were a good captain," continued Craig. "Kind of freaked on me, but then . . . he asked me why I thought that. I said you got the room going before the game."

Aiden glanced at Craig. *Was this for real?*

"What you did wasn't *that* bad," Craig said, rolling his eyes. "You were just trying to get extra ice time. My dad gets ice for me, but he said you didn't buy yours and he does. That's what made him the maddest."

"I shouldn't have gone on the ice," said Aiden. "I get that I was wrong."

"It's okay with me, but my dad doesn't agree. He thinks it was wrong. But hey, good on you for wanting extra practice," Craig said, smirking, but in a good way.

Aiden nudged Craig with his shoulder. "Just trying to be as good as you."

"Never, dude. Never."

"Hey," said Aiden quietly. "Please don't say anything to the team. I want to tell everyone at practice."

"Sure. Your call."

Mr. Rowland stood in the doorway and gave them his perfected one eyebrow up, one eyebrow down look. When Aiden went by him, Mr. Rowland said, "I read your outline. You're good to go — but this is the last one."

"Thanks," said Aiden.

"Beat you to your desk," said Craig.

Aiden took off running, but Craig knocked him sideways. They both burst out laughing.

* * *

In English, the last period of the day, they had time to work on their essays. Aiden bowed his head and wrote furiously. Now he really had a story to write.

"Boy, I've never seen you work so hard," said Susie. She had turned around to talk to him.

"I changed my topic," said Aiden.

"What are you writing about now?"

"Ned."

"Wow! Good for you for switching." She gave him a thumbs-up. "Way better topic. I didn't want to say anything, but your Florida one sucked. I mean, the differences between what you wear going to practice? Shorts versus pants? Come on. So bad."

"Okay, okay," said Aiden.

"I think my brother is coming Saturday. He's the one I'm writing my paper on. He's such a dude. But he might have to wear headphones because he hates loud noises."

"I'd like to read it when you're finished," said Aiden. "I'm calling mine 'My Friend Ned.'"

"That's a great title! Before we hand in the final, final essays, we should read each other's and make comments so we both get good marks."

"I'm a lousy speller," said Aiden.

"We'll work on that one. I'm a lousy baker, so we're kind of even."

"They don't even relate." Aiden shook his head, hiding his smile.

"Practice today! Then it's tournament time! Life is grandioso!" Susie clapped her hands.

Practice. Aiden's stomach twirled like a spinny ride, making him feel sick. He stared down at his paper, but all the lines blurred together. For once, he dreaded the final bell.

* * *

The dressing room was empty when Aiden pushed the door open and walked in. He sat down and leaned against the wall. He had thought over and over about what he should say to the team. Aiden was running through it again when the door opened and Coach Ira came in. He sat down beside Aiden on the bench.

"You want me to speak to the guys for you?" Coach Ira asked.

Aiden shook his head. "I have to do this."

"I'm sorry, Mallory. You really deserve to wear the 'C.'" He sighed. "This is such a mess. I didn't think being a coach would be this hard."

"I'm not sure all teams are like this one," said Aiden.

Coach Ira ran his hand through his curls. "When I was your age, hockey was always so much fun."

"It'll be okay," said Aiden, rubbing his hands together. "We've had lots of fun." He couldn't stop thinking about how he had to talk to the team. He'd already sweated through one T-shirt.

Coach Ira gave Aiden a little pat on the shoulder. "If you need help, let me know."

The team piled in and the chatter was loud. Aiden's throat dried up. He kept swallowing to keep it open. *What if it closed when he tried to talk?* Everyone else seemed so excited about the tournament, and even about the bake sale. Manny's mom had already been baking and was freezing the cookies so they would stay fresh. Aiden wished he could join in on the excitement, but all he wanted to do was run to a toilet and barf.

Finally the team was dressed, and the coaches came in with Susie and Audrey.

"Listen up," said Coach Ira. Quiet filled the room.

"We've had to make a change to our captains." Coach Ira glanced at Aiden and nodded.

Aiden stood up, his legs shaking. "I'm, um, so sorry but I can, uh, no longer be the captain of the team." He sucked in a huge breath. This was it. He had to say why. "I snuck on the ice with Ned early in the mornings for extra practice, and we weren't supposed to. It cost the arena extra money, and I shouldn't have done it. Not being captain anymore is part of my punishment."

"What?" Susie stared wide-eyed at Aiden. "That doesn't sound bad enough to take your 'C' away. People do *way worse* things than that."

"Yeah," said Bilal. "They do." He hung his head.

The team started talking, the noise escalating. Coach Ben put his fingers in his mouth and let out one of his shrill whistles. Aiden had already sat down. He'd said what he wanted to say. His legs were still shaking.

"Can I say something?" said Bilal in a shaky voice. He'd never stood up and said anything in the room before.

"Go ahead," said Coach Ira.

"Aiden is our leader. Our captain. Even if they took

it away, I think he should still be our captain. Can we do that?"

Aiden couldn't believe his ears. Had Bilal really just said that?

Colin stood up. "I agree."

"Me too," said Manny. He held up his stick. "He helped me tape this baby!"

The noise rose again as everyone started to talk in favour of Aiden being captain. Aiden was shocked. Then suddenly everyone started chanting.

"MAL-LO-RY! MAL-LO-RY!"

Coach Ira held up his hands, and this time Coach Ben didn't need to whistle, because the room instantly went silent.

"I agree," said Coach Ira, "but we do need someone to wear the 'C' on the ice to deal with the refs. Aiden can be your captain in the dressing room, and I'm totally cool with that. Does everyone agree?"

The entire team — even Craig — put up their hands.

"Great, problem solved. Now, as for who wears the 'C' on their jersey. Us coaches aren't picking this time, and we are not doing a re-vote," said Coach Ira. "We have taken your votes from before, and we will cross off Aiden's name for now, and just go with who got the most votes. Jory, you will now wear the 'C.' Susie, you are still 'A.' And Mason, you have the second 'A.'"

Aiden stole a glance at Craig and saw him lower his head and pretend to tie his laces.

"Okay, let's get on the ice," said Coach Ira.

Ten minutes into practice, Aiden heard Mr. O'Brien call Craig over. They were in the middle of a skating drill, and Mr. O'Brien's constant calling of Craig's name was impossible for anyone to ignore.

Aiden heard Coach Ira mutter to Coach Ben, "Not this guy again. I thought they said he couldn't come to our practices anymore."

Of course, Craig finally gave in to his father's demands and skated over to him. After a few seconds, Craig skated back out to the ice, his shoulders slumped. His father stormed over to the bench.

"Coach, can I have a word with you?"

"After practice," said Coach Ira.

"Your assistant can run your practice. Or my kid can. Because he should be captain."

Coach Ira blew out a huge rush of air and ran his hands through his mop of hair. "Ben, run the drill." He skated over to where Mr. O'Brien was standing.

The practice continued, and as Aiden skated around the cones, he could hear Mr. O'Brien yelling about how Craig should be captain. Getting rid of Aiden wearing the "C" hadn't helped; Craig still wasn't captain and he was still on the three team.

Coach Ira kept repeating that he went strictly with the votes.

Suddenly Mr. O'Brien jumped over the boards onto the ice and grabbed Coach Ira by the jacket.

"Dad! Don't!" yelled Craig. "Leave him alone."

"Stay out of this!"

"Why do you have to wreck everything!" Craig headed to the bench.

"Leave me alone," said Coach Ira. He struggled to pull Mr. O'Brien's hands off his collar. "Let go of me, man." Then he called out, "Ben, call the cops!"

"You little punk," said Mr. O'Brien. He lifted his fist like he was going to slug him.

"Len!" Mr. Ramos showed up from somewhere and moved quickly toward the altercation. "You are out of hand. Let go of him. I want you out of the arena. Now!"

Mr. O'Brien dropped his hands. Coach Ira rubbed his neck and said to Mr. Ramos, "I don't want him in the rink when I'm here or else I will call the cops."

"I understand. I'm sorry," said Mr. Ramos. "Is there anything else you need?"

"No, but if he comes near me again, this will become a police matter."

"He won't. I promise you that."

Coach Ira turned to the team. "I'm sorry you had

to see that." Then he looked around. "Where's Craig?"

Aiden searched the bench, but Craig was gone. "He must be in the dressing room," Aiden said.

"Ben, run practice," said Coach Ira.

Five minutes later, when they were well into their breakout drill, Coach Ira came back on the ice with Craig.

"Let's end with a scrimmage," yelled Coach Ira.

By now everyone knew the rotation of the scrimmage that ended the practice. As Aiden skated to the bench to sit for the first shift, he went by Craig. He gave him a quick pat on the shoulder and kept moving. Craig kept his head down.

CHAPTER TWENTY–FIVE

LUKE MALLORY MEMORIAL

When Aiden walked into the arena that Friday night, the lobby was buzzing. So many people had shown up! Aiden thought it looked like the entire town was there.

All of the silent-auction items were laid out on tables, and people were milling around, writing down numbers. The items looked fantastic. Aiden's mother had helped wrap them in Cellophane with bows. There were books, T-shirts, baskets full of blankets and gift certificates. There was tons of hockey equipment, and even a barbecue and a snow blower! There was also all his dad's stuff that his mother had donated, and Aiden's photo of Sidney Crosby that he'd taken off his wall. It was like the entire town had chipped in to help the arena.

Off to the side was a table with a red tablecloth. Behind the table was the poster that Susie had made, only blown up way bigger. That's where they were setting up for the bake sale as soon as their first game was over.

The sight of the people talking and laughing filled Aiden with energy. He glanced around, smiling, and his gaze stopped on the framed picture of his father in his

Florida Panthers jersey, which was sitting on an easel. He slowly walked over to it. Once he was standing in front of it, he dropped his bag.

"This is all for you, Dad. For all you did," Aiden whispered under his breath.

I'm so proud of you, Bud. You know that, right?

"I do. I screwed up, but it's okay now."

Yeah, you learned. It will help you be stronger.

Suddenly Aiden felt someone beside him. He turned and saw his mother. She linked her arm in his and he let her. "This is something," she said.

"It sure is," said Aiden.

She leaned into him and whispered, "I'm bidding on all of those jerseys I donated. I want them back."

Aiden laughed. "I brought my allowance money," he said. "I'm buying a T-shirt."

"Me too," said his mother. "We can be twins."

"Okay, Mom, that's not gonna happen." Then he stood tall. "I gotta go," he said. "I'm still captain of the room, which means I need to be first in the dressing room."

"Your dad would be so proud of you."

"I know." Aiden smiled.

When Aiden got to the dressing room, he took out his ball and started shooting against the wall. Pretty soon the room started filling up, and today everyone had as much enthusiasm as Susie. They were all there except Craig. He was a no-show, but Aiden knew why.

Once Susie and Audrey were in the room, the coaches spoke to the team. "There's a little change to our lineup today," said Coach Ira. "Craig has been called up to play for the two team, and chances are he will remain there for the duration of the season."

A rumour had been swirling that Mr. O'Brien had been banned from entering the arena for a year because of his attack on Coach Ira. This gave Craig a chance to be on the team he should have made from the beginning. Word was the coach wanted him as long as he didn't have to have his dad.

Coach Ira stopped talking and smiled at a boy named Logan. Aiden recognized him from school. "I would like to welcome Logan to our team tonight. He has been called up for today's game."

Logan didn't say a word, nor did he smile, and his leg was going up and down at a hundred miles an hour. Aiden recognized that movement — and he also knew what he had to do.

"Welcome to Team Chaos," said Aiden. "Our slogan is we're chaos on the ice where it matters."

Logan gave a nervous laugh.

"Thanks for that, Aiden," said Coach Ira. "Listen up. Here are the lines for today." He glanced at his phone. "For consistency, I'd like to keep the Jacob, Deke and Henry line together. Aiden, you now will centre between Jory and Bilal. Susie, I'd like to try you at centre with J.J. and Logan. I know you played some centre last year. Defence will rotate. Audrey, you will start tonight, and Tree, you will play the second half."

"We ready, team?" Coach Ira held up his hands.

"We're ready, Coach," said Aiden.

The coaches left the room, and Aiden stood up. "We may be missing O'Brien, but we can do this if we play like a team. Let's play our game, and play hard! Battle for every puck. Don't give up. And be chaos on the ice. Let's beat those Grimwood Knights, and let's win this tournament! Time for a Chaos cheer!"

Hands stretched out to the middle of the dressing room. They chanted, "We're chaos on the ice where it matters! Go, Chaos!"

Aiden looked Logan in the eyes and smiled before he said, "Now let's kick some butt!"

The team filed out. Coach Ira started Jacob's line, and Aiden sat beside Jory on the bench. The play went up and down the ice with neither team having any scoring chances.

"I'm happy for O.B.," Jory said.

"Me too," said Aiden.

"Off the faceoff," said Jory, "if you push it forward, I'll attack."

Aiden held up his gloved hand, and Jory hit it with his.

"Line change," said Coach Ira. "Aiden's line, go!"

"Come on," Aiden said to Jory. "Let's do some damage." He hopped over the boards.

The puck dropped. Aiden swatted at it, pushing it forward and through the other centre's legs. Jory darted around his man and picked up the puck. Like a fly, Bilal buzzed forward. He hit the net and Jory fired him a pass. Bilal tried to tap it in but missed. Aiden scooted behind the net to pick up the puck and saw Bilal over on the wall. They'd practised this. Bilal was about to get hammered by someone twice his size, even though there was no checking. But it didn't happen. He squeaked underneath and Aiden rifled off the pass. Bilal picked it up.

Jory tapped his stick on the ice and Bilal passed to him. Jory one-timed it but the Grimwood goalie made a spectacular glove save.

"You were robbed," said Aiden, as they skated to the faceoff circle.

Again Aiden won the draw but this time he sent the puck back to Finn. Finn fumbled with it, but Mason went behind and retrieved it. Aiden's line hemmed in their opponents and cycled the puck. From Finn to Mason to Aiden to Bilal to Jory. Finally the puck landed on Aiden's stick for the third time, and he had an open lane. He took two strides and was going to do a wrist shot, but then remembered his work with Ned.

Aiden shovelled the puck from his forehand to his backhand and beat the goalie on his glove-hand side. The red light shone.

"Great goal," said Jory.

"Ned taught me that," said Aiden.

The score remained 1–0 for the rest of the first period. Then Grimwood tied it up in the second period, on a goal that Audrey didn't have a chance at. It was a hard shot from the blueline, by a big defenceman who could just blast it from the point.

The game continued into the third period, and the action was non-stop back and forth.

"Aiden's line, you're up," said Coach Ira.

Aiden looked at the clock. There were just three minutes left, and it was still tied.

"Let's do this," he said. He headed to the faceoff circle. When the ref dropped the puck, Aiden tried to poke it through the other centre's legs, but he quickly put his skate blades together.

"I'm on to you," the player said. Then he picked up the puck before Aiden could and fired off a pass to his winger.

Aiden twisted around as fast as he could and skated down the ice. He saw Jory racing beside him and Bilal busting down the other side. Manny faced a two-on-one.

The Grimwood player wound up before Aiden could get there. Tree crouched in anticipation.

Suddenly Manny dove just as the shot was blasted toward the net. The puck cracked against his stick and went careening into the corner. Aiden rushed in, beating Grimwood to the loose puck. Manny was still getting up when Aiden wheeled around the back of the net and flipped the puck up to Jory.

Jory raced up the ice with Bilal. He had a little opening on his side, but Bilal was now in perfect position for a pass. Jory sent the puck over and Bilal snapped at it. It hit the goalie's pads and rebounded out. Jory swooped in and gave the loose puck a tap. The goalie tried but it slipped under his pads and into the back of the net.

Jory jumped on his skates.

Aiden joined the huddle. "Holy moly," said Manny. "What a snipe!"

"That was such a good block," Jory said to Manny, tapping his helmet. "Where'd you learn that?

"Hockey highlights," said Manny. "NHL players do it all the time. Do you know they even have stats for blocked shots?"

Aiden laughed. "Keep watching those highlights, Manny."

The game ended with Chaos winning 2–1. Maybe they hadn't won like they did when Craig was with them, but they had still won, and everyone had contributed. Coach Ira and Coach Ben were ecstatic on the bench, jumping up and down like they'd just won a huge championship. Aiden laughed knowing they still had to win two more games to come top in their pool. **Then** came a semifinal and the gold-medal game!

In the dressing room everyone was pumped about the win and excited for their game the next morning. When the guys were dressed in their suits, Coach Ira came in with Susie and Audrey. He was holding on to an ugly gold hat with "Chaos" written in sparkles across the front.

"Every game of the tournament we are going to pick a player who deserves this hat. And if you win, you have to wear it out of the dressing room," said Coach Ira.

The guys laughed. Susie said, "Coach, it has sparkles, and we're a hockey team."

"I *wanna* win it," said Jory.

"Today . . ." Coach Ira continued, ". . . drum roll please . . ." The drum roll started, and it was so loud Coach Ira had to yell. ". . . the hat goes to Mr. Manny for that outrageously wild dive. Way to take one for the team."

The team erupted into cheers. Manny looked like he might cry.

When he had the hat sitting lopsided on his head, Manny said, "It didn't actually hit me, but I guess if it did it would have hurt."

On the way out of the dressing room, Coach Ira high-fived everyone. This time Aiden really slapped his hand back. Coach Ira looked so happy and his face was beaming.

"That was a fun win," he said to Aiden. "I think I do like coaching."

Aiden held up his thumb. "That was totally fun," he said, and kept walking down the hall.

As the Zamboni cleaned the ice for the next game, Aiden helped set up the bake-sale table, although Susie was on her game and bossing everyone around. She'd even made a spreadsheet to record their sales.

When everything was ready, he turned to Susie. "I'll be right back. I've got something I gotta do."

Aiden scanned the arena. When he saw Ned, he walked over to him.

"Hey, Ned," said Aiden.

"What a game!" said Ned. "Wowee."

Aiden pulled a puck from his jacket and handed it to

Ned. On the puck, he'd written in silver marker, "First Ned Backhand Goal!"

"This is for me?" Ned asked.

"Target practice paid off."

"Two Mallory pucks," said Ned. "I'll put them . . . side by side."

Aiden liked the thought of that — his puck beside his dad's.

"I'm going to do some maintenance around the arena tomorrow," said Aiden. "I'll be helping you with the outdoor ice. Soon we can get back to practising."

"I heard you were helping me." Ned looked sheepish.

Aiden held up his fist. "We're a team."

Ned didn't fist bump back, though, because he was touching the puck Aiden had given him like it was valuable.

"See you tomorrow," Aiden said to Ned, as he saw his mother waving to him from across the room.

"You betcha. Thanks for the puck," said Ned.

Aiden walked over to his mom, who was holding a big bag.

"That was a great game," she said. "Maybe you'll even win the tournament."

"That'd be so sweet," said Aiden. And it would be, but only time would tell. He pointed to the bag. "What's in there?"

His mother's smile stretched across her face. "I got all of Dad's jerseys back. Cost me a few dollars, but whatever."

Aiden laughed. "Good for you."

"Did you end up using your allowance to buy an inaugural tournament T-shirt?"

Aiden shook his head and gave her a silly smile. "Nope. I'm buying a video game instead."

"What?"

He shrugged, and put his hand over his heart. "I don't need to wear a T-shirt with Dad's face on it. I'm just going to take some of Ned's advice and wear him here."

ACKNOWLEDGEMENTS

There are so many people involved in getting a book published. It's very much like all the people involved in putting a hockey team together. It all starts off with a general manager who sees the talent and decides they like the project, but then has to make everyone believe that this is the right choice. For being a wonderful general manager, I thank Erin O'Connor. She was the first champion for *Taking the Ice*, the first one to see there was potential. Once she pitched and it was accepted, she passed the project on to my coach, Erin Haggett. I call them Team Erin! Erin H. went through the drills with me and helped me make this book ready to play. Thank you for being so detailed, efficient and encouraging, all signs of an effective coach. All head coaches need strong people to help them out, and in publishing there are many involved. Tamara Sztainbok, thank you for being that fabulous trainer and proofing the book. Stella Partheniou Grasso, thank you for keeping everyone on track at team meetings. And to Maral Maclagan — rights and contracts manager — for getting all the necessary paperwork done.

Sometimes, a book needs some extra dryland training. I thank Erica Taylor, M.A., C. Psych., a child psychologist who helped with Aiden. My brother, John Schultz, M.D., also helped give advice on Aiden's anxiety. Amanda Wagner, Ph.D., is a neuropsychologist from the Child Mind Institute and was an expert reader for the character of Ned.

Then there's Diane Kerner, who makes a great leader of an organization. Thank you, Diane, for allowing your staff to work their magic, and for adding your editorial advice when needed. You know how to get the best from everyone.

Once the words in the book are in shape and ready to play, there are always the game-day people who work behind the scenes to make sure the experience is fun for the fans. Or in this case . . . the readers. Khaula Mazhar, thank you for making such a beautiful cover (in hockey you'd be designing the jersey logo). Andrea Casault, thank you for your art direction in making sure this is a beautiful product. And to Denise Anderson, Nikole Kritikos and Cali Platek for marketing and publicity, making sure everyone knows about the book and wants to read it. You make sure the readers/fans are excited for release day.

Like athletes, authors need agents, and I thank mine. Amy Tompkins, from the Transatlantic Agency, you are so valued for all the work you do to read, give advice, get the contracts signed and to take care of any endorsements.

When it's time for puck drop . . . fans are important to games, and readers are important to books. I thank you, my readers! I write for you. Please, enjoy!!

ABOUT THE AUTHOR

Lorna Schultz Nicholson grew up in St. Catharines, Ontario, and as a child loved to read, write and compete in all kinds of sports. She played defence on the St. Catharines girls' all-star hockey team and was a member of the Canadian national rowing team. She earned a degree in human performance from the University of Victoria, where she also coached rowing. Lorna has worked in television and radio broadcasting, as well as written magazine articles and columns. Now, Lorna is thrilled that she has been able to combine her passion for books with her love of sport — she is the respected author of many middle-grade and YA novels, as well as the Amazing Hockey Stories biography series. Lorna is the proud mother of three and lives in Edmonton, Alberta, with her husband, Bob, and dogs Molly and Poncho. Not surprisingly, she is a HUGE Edmonton Oilers fan.